Disney Fairies

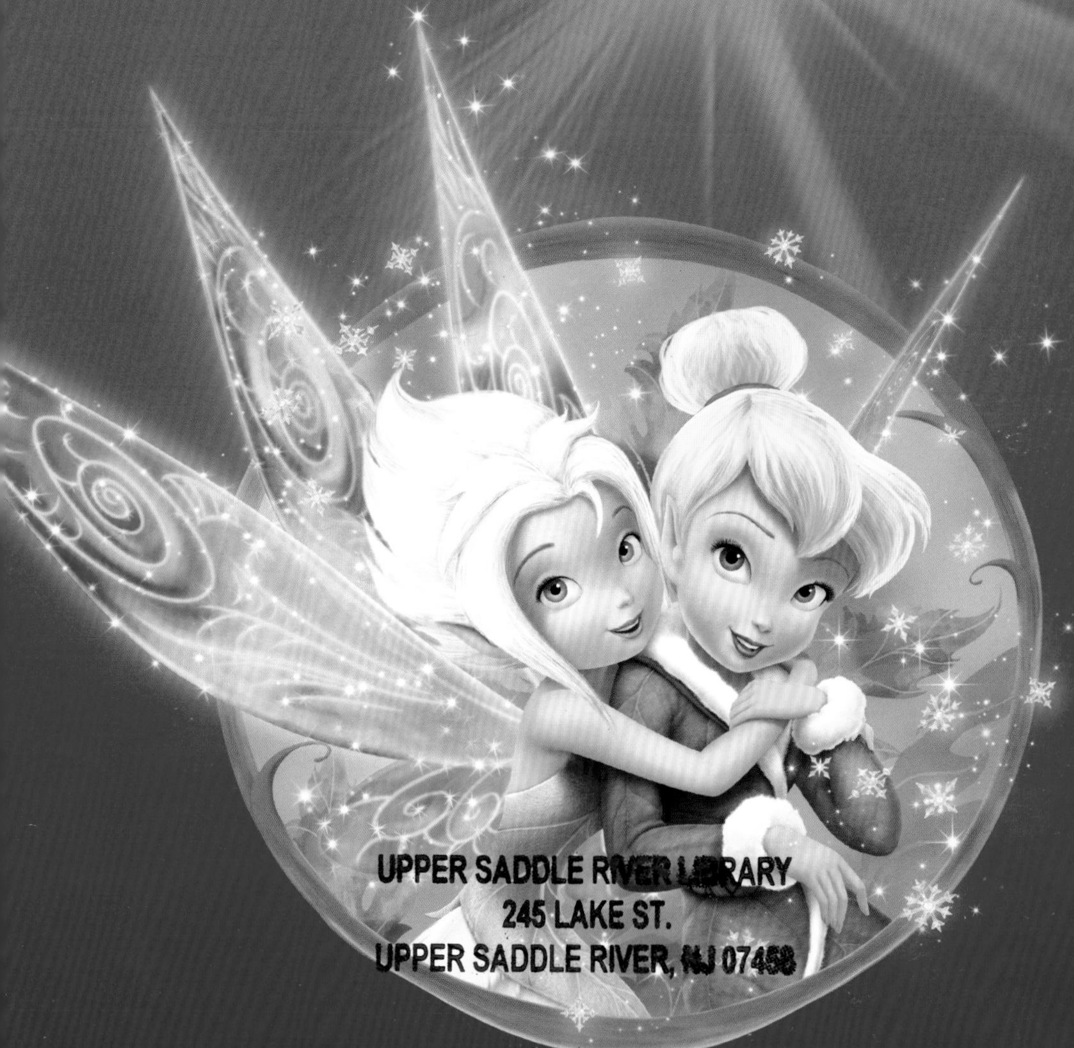

PAPERCUTZ™

Disney Fairies

Graphic Novels Available from PAPERCUTZ

FAIRIES
Prilla's Talent

Graphic Novel #1
"Prilla's Talent"

FAIRIES

Graphic Novel #2
"Tinker Bell and the Wings of Rani"

FAIRIES

Graphic Novel #3
"Tinker Bell and the Day of the Dragon"

FAIRIES
Tinker Bell to the Rescue

Graphic Novel #4
"Tinker Bell to the Rescue"

FAIRIES

Graphic Novel #5
"Tinker Bell and the Pirate Adventure"

FAIRIES
A Present for Tinker Bell

Graphic Novel #6
"A Present for Tinker Bell"

FAIRIES

Graphic Novel #7
"Tinker Bell the Perfect Fairy"

FAIRIES
Tinker Bell

Graphic Novel #8
"Tinker Bell and her Stories for a Rainy Day"

TinkerBell

Graphic Novel #9
"Tinker Bell and her Magical Arrival"

Disney
FAIRIES
Tinker Bell

Graphic Novel #10
"Tinker Bell and the Lucky Rainbow"

Disney
FAIRIES

Graphic Novel #11
"Tinker Bell and the Most Precious Gift"

TinkerBell

Graphic Novel #12
"Tinker Bell and the Lost Treasure"

TinkerBell

Graphic Novel #13
"Tinker Bell and the Pixie Hollow Games"

Tinker Bell

Graphic Novel #14
"Tinker Bell and Blaze"

TinkerBell

Tinker Bell and the Great Fairy Rescue

TinkerBell

Graphic Novel #15
"Tinker Bell and the Secret of the Wings"

DISNEY FAIRIES graphic novels are available in paperback for $7.99 each; in hardcover for $12.99 each except #5, $6.99PB, $10.99HC. #6-14 are $7.99PB $11.99HC. Tinker Bell and the Great Fairy Rescue is $9.99 in hardcover only.
Available at booksellers everywhere.

See more at papercutz.com

Or you can order from us: Please add $4.00 for postage and handling for first book, and add $1.00 for each additional book. Please make check payable to NBM Publishing. Send to: Papercutz, 160 Broadway, Suite 700, East Wing, New York, NY 10038 or call 800 886 1223 (9-6 EST M-F) MC-Visa-Amex accepted.

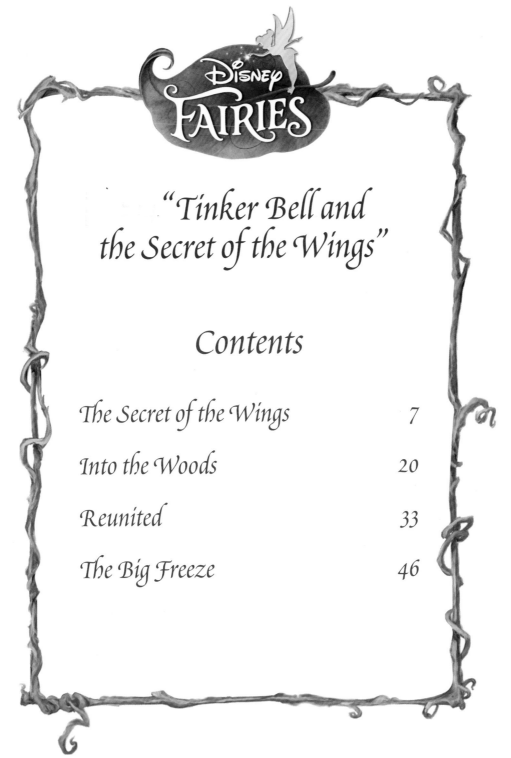

"Tinker Bell and the Secret of the Wings"

Contents

PAPERCUTZ

NEW YORK

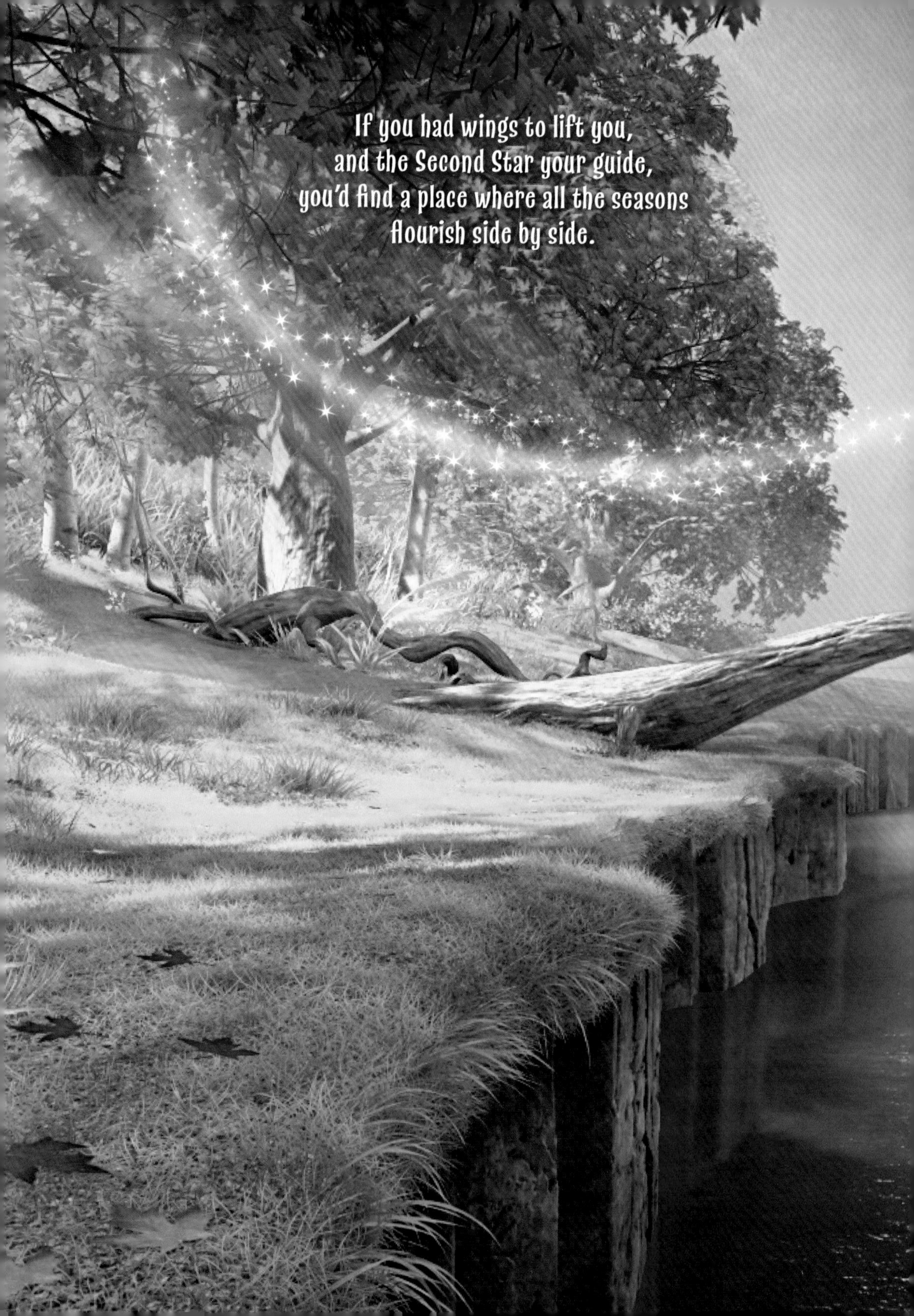

If you had wings to lift you,
and the Second Star your guide,
you'd find a place where all the seasons
flourish side by side.

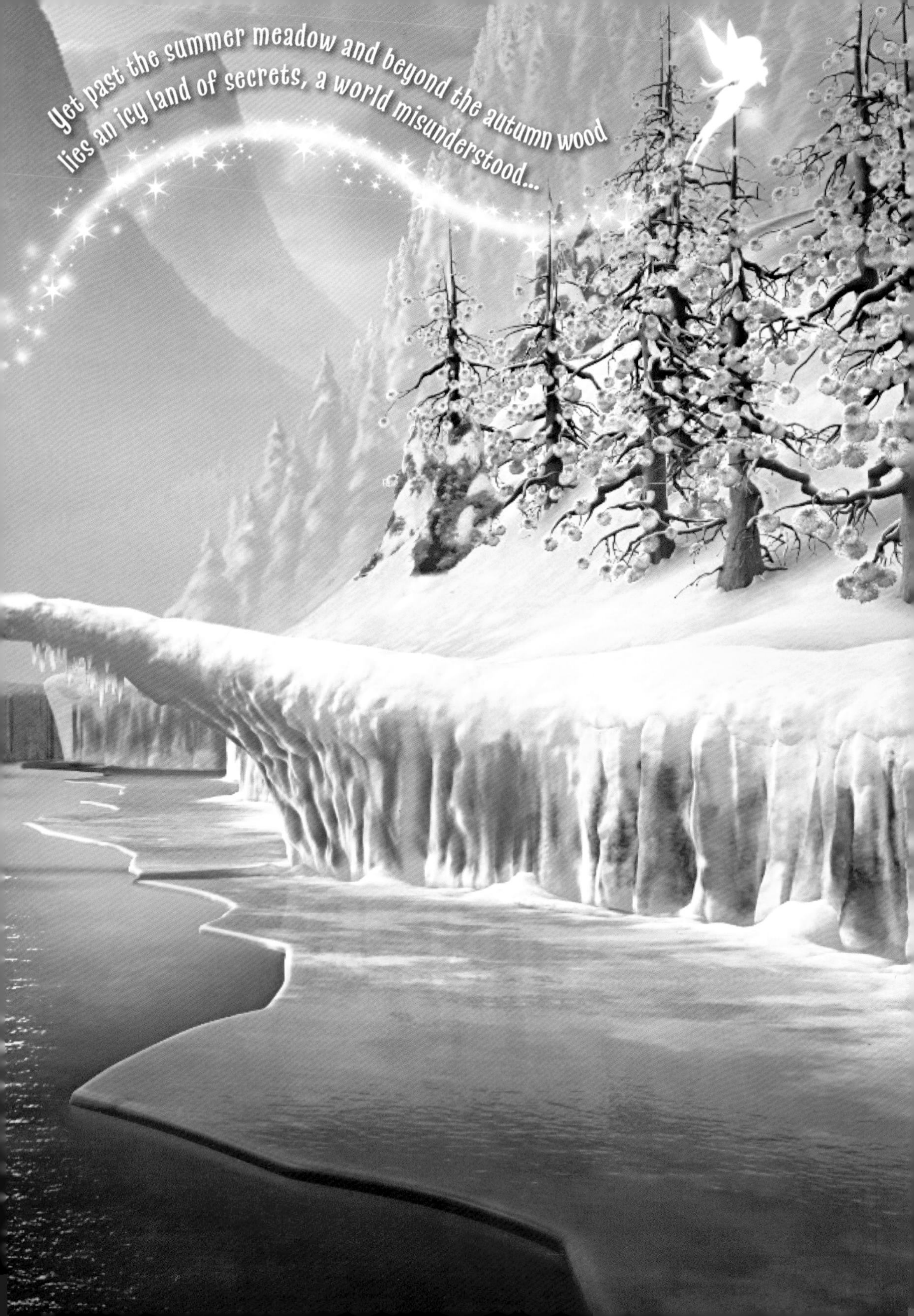

Yet past the summer meadow and beyond the autumn wood
lies an icy land of secrets, a world misunderstood...

"The Secret of the Wings"
Script: Tea Orsi
(Based on the screenplay by Bobs Gannaway & Peggy Holmes, and
Ryan Rowe, and Tom Rogers. Creative development by Vicki Letizia)
Revised Captions: Cortney Faye Powell and Jim Salicrup
Layout: Marino Gentile, Fernando Güell
Pencils: Sara Storino, Gianluca Barone, Michela Frare;
Inks: Cristina Giorgilli, Francesco Abrignani, Michela Frare;
Color: Kawai Studio
Letters: Janice Chiang
Page 7 Art:
Concept: Tea Orsi
Pencils: Sara Storino
Color: Gianluca Barone, Andrea Cagol

"Reunited"
Script: Tea Orsi
(Based on the screenplay by Bobs Gannaway & Peggy Holmes, and
Ryan Rowe, and Tom Rogers. Creative development by Vicki Letizia)
Revised Captions: Cortney Faye Powell and Jim Salicrup
Layout: Marino Gentile, Fernando Güell
Pencils: Sara Storino, Gianluca Barone, Michela Frare;
Inks: Cristina Giorgilli, Francesco Abrignani, Michela Frare;
Color: Kawai Studio
Letters: Janice Chiang
Page 33 Art:
Concept: Tea Orsi
Pencils and Inks: Sara Storino
Color: Andrea Cagol

"Into the Woods"
Script: Tea Orsi
(Based on the screenplay by Bobs Gannaway & Peggy Holmes, and
Ryan Rowe, and Tom Rogers. Creative development by Vicki Letizia)
Revised Captions: Cortney Faye Powell and Jim Salicrup
Layout: Marino Gentile, Fernando Güell
Pencils: Sara Storino, Gianluca Barone, Michela Frare;
Inks: Cristina Giorgilli, Francesco Abrignani, Michela Frare;
Color: Kawai Studio
Letters: Janice Chiang
Page 20 Art:
Concept: Tea Orsi
Pencils and Inks: Sara Storino
Color: Andrea Cagol

"The Big Freeze"
Script: Tea Orsi
(Based on the screenplay by Bobs Gannaway & Peggy Holmes, and
Ryan Rowe, and Tom Rogers. Creative development by Vicki Letizia)
Revised Captions: Cortney Faye Powell and Jim Salicrup
Layout: Marino Gentile, Fernando Güell
Pencils: Sara Storino, Gianluca Barone, Michela Frare;
Inks: Cristina Giorgilli, Francesco Abrignani, Michela Frare;
Color: Kawai Studio
Letters: Janice Chiang
Page 46 Art:
Concept: Tea Orsi
Pencils and Inks: Sara Storino
Color: Andrea Cagol

Production – Dawn K. Guzzo
Special Thanks – Shiho Tilley and John Tanzer
Production Coordinator – Beth Scorzato
Associate Editor – Michael Petranek
Jim Salicrup
Editor-in-Chief

ISBN: 978-1-59707-729-3 paperback edition
ISBN: 978-1-59707-730-9 hardcover edition

Printed in China
July 2014 by Asia One Printing LTD
13/F Asia One Tower
8 Fung Yip St., Chaiwan
Hong Kong

Papercutz books may be purchased for business or promotional use. For information on bulk purchases please contact Macmillan
Corporate and Premium Sales Department at (800) 221-7945 x5442.

Distributed by Macmillan
First Papercutz Printing

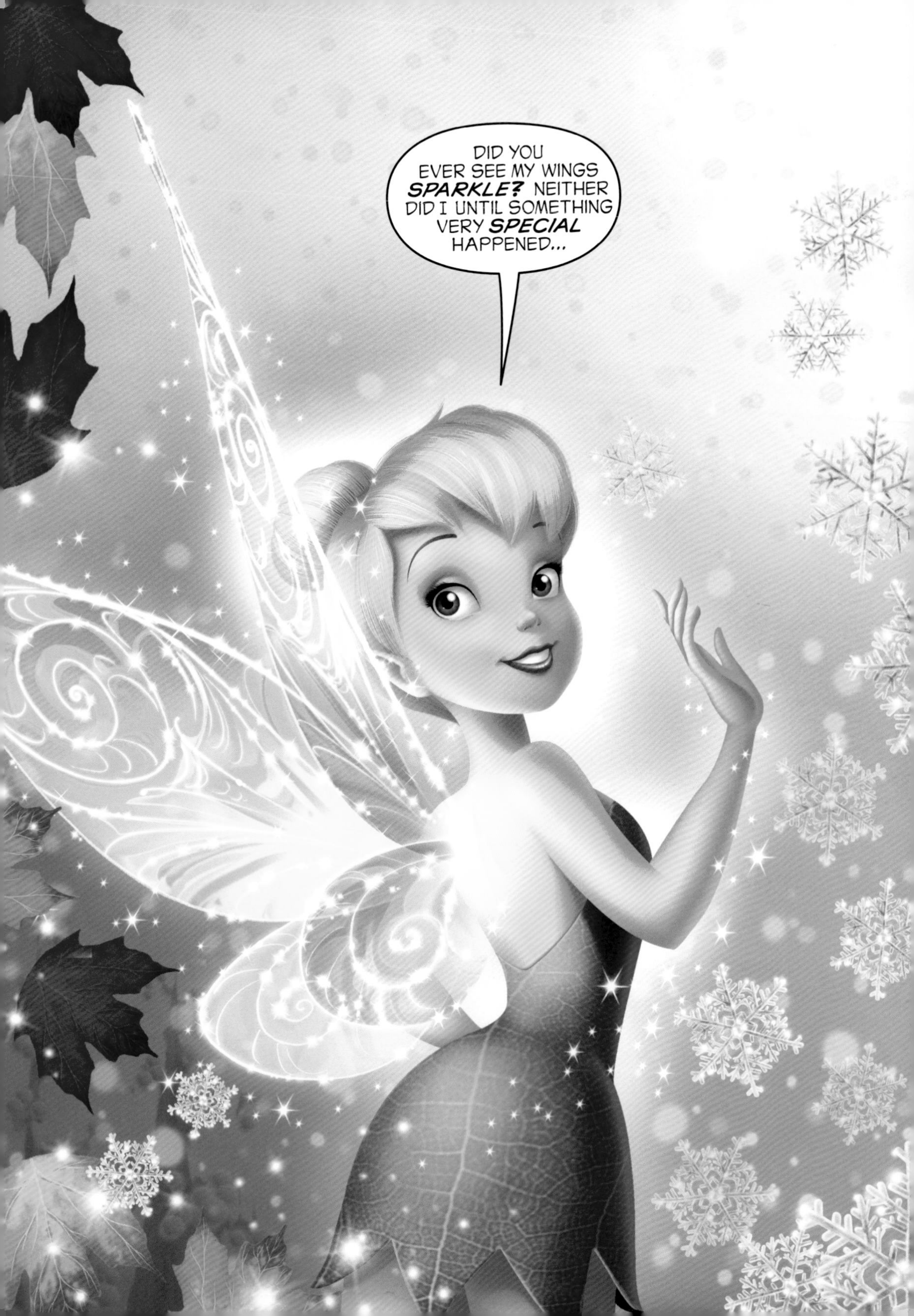
DID YOU EVER SEE MY WINGS ***SPARKLE?*** NEITHER DID I UNTIL SOMETHING VERY ***SPECIAL*** HAPPENED...

THE SECRET OF THE WINGS

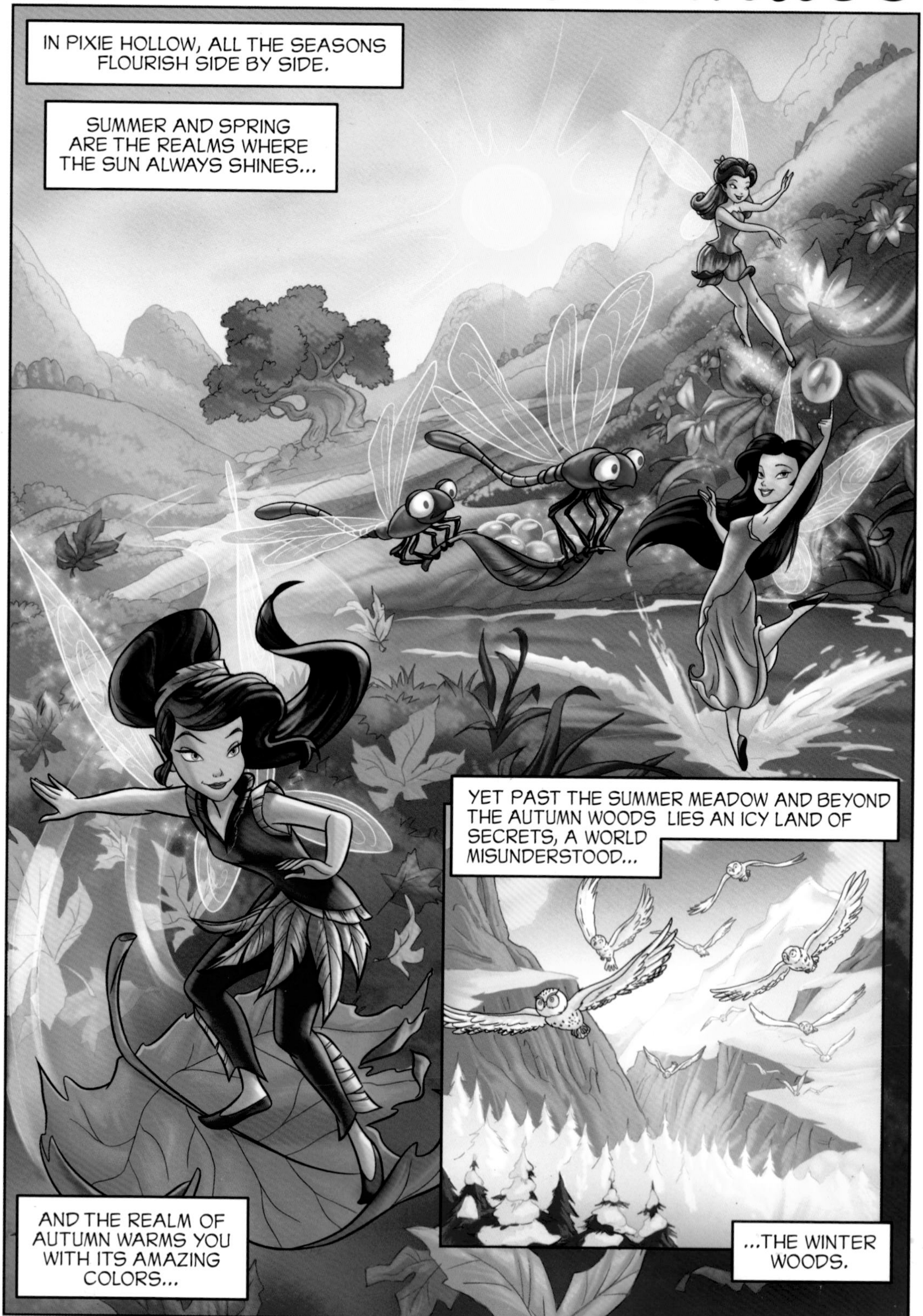

IN PIXIE HOLLOW, ALL THE SEASONS FLOURISH SIDE BY SIDE.
SUMMER AND SPRING ARE THE REALMS WHERE THE SUN ALWAYS SHINES...
AND THE REALM OF AUTUMN WARMS YOU WITH ITS AMAZING COLORS...
YET PAST THE SUMMER MEADOW AND BEYOND THE AUTUMN WOODS LIES AN ICY LAND OF SECRETS, A WORLD MISUNDERSTOOD...
...THE WINTER WOODS.

TODAY, IN PIXIE HOLLOW, THE TINKER FAIRIES ARE HELPING OUT THE WINTER FAIRIES, EVEN THOUGH THEY'VE NEVER MET EACH OTHER...

LOOK SHARP, EVERYONE! THE *SNOWY OWLS* WILL SOON BE ARRIVING TO TAKE THE *SNOWFLAKE BASKETS* TO THE WINTER WOODS.

OH, BASKET WEAVING IS MY FAVORITE THING, BOBBLE!

REALLY? I'M PARTIAL TO MACRAME.

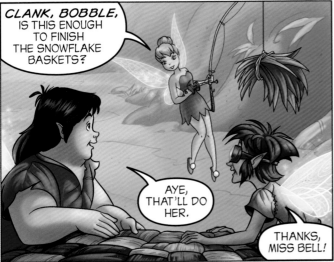

CLANK, BOBBLE, IS THIS ENOUGH TO FINISH THE SNOWFLAKE BASKETS?

AYE, THAT'LL DO HER.

THANKS, MISS BELL!

I CAN'T BELIEVE WE MAKE THE BASKETS BUT DON'T GET TO TAKE THEM TO THE WINTER FAIRIES!

I MEAN WOULDN'T YOU WANT TO GO INTO THE *WINTER WOODS?*

NO! WE WOULDN'T LAST A DAY IN THAT *COLD!*

BESIDES, I'M AFRAID OF GLACIERS!

THEY'RE KNOWN FOR THEIR STEALTH!

GLACIERS?

BUT SUDDENLY...

AARROOOO

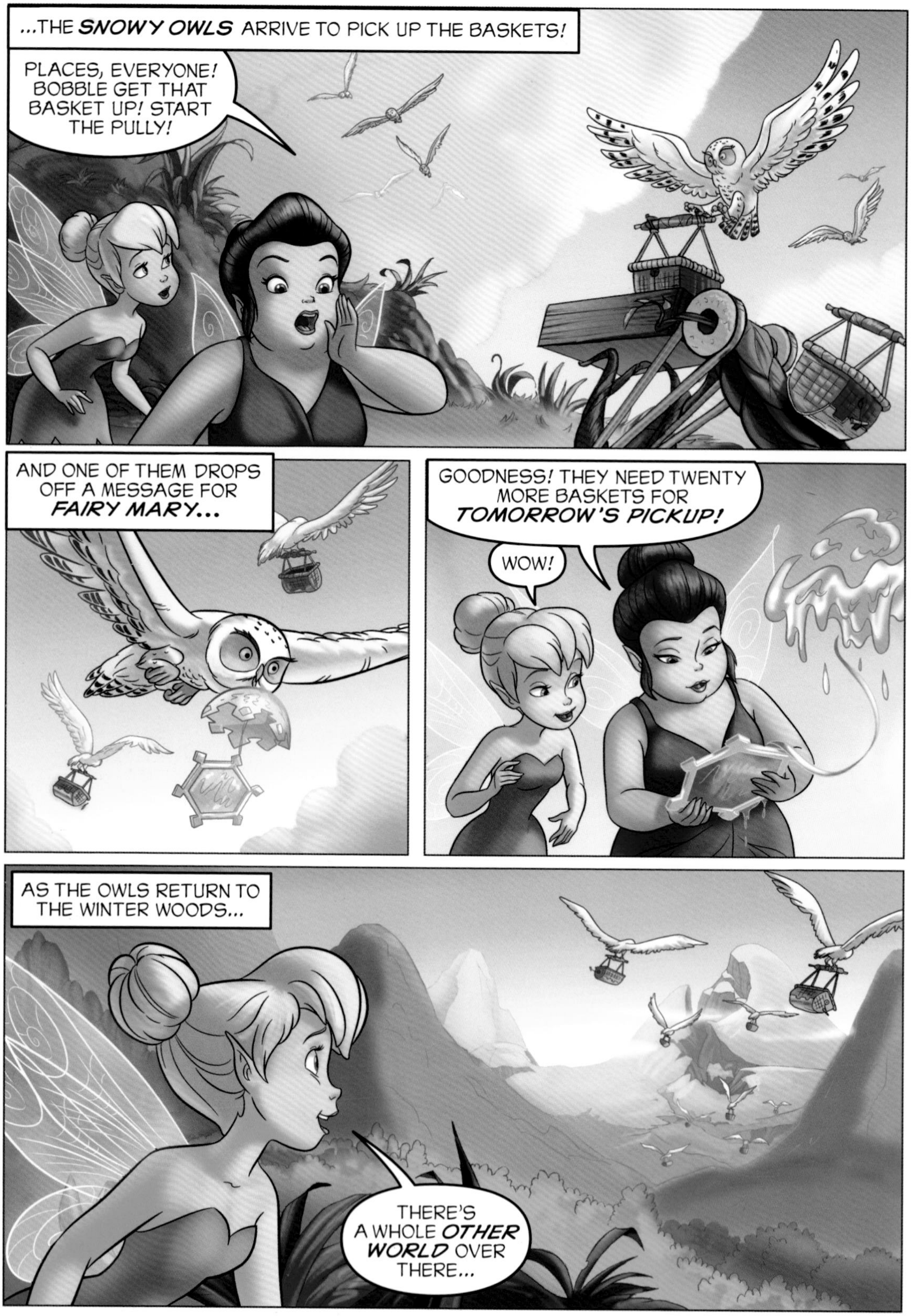
...THE SNOWY OWLS ARRIVE TO PICK UP THE BASKETS!
PLACES, EVERYONE! BOBBLE GET THAT BASKET UP! START THE PULLY!
AND ONE OF THEM DROPS OFF A MESSAGE FOR FAIRY MARY...
GOODNESS! THEY NEED TWENTY MORE BASKETS FOR TOMORROW'S PICKUP!
WOW!
AS THE OWLS RETURN TO THE WINTER WOODS...
THERE'S A WHOLE OTHER WORLD OVER THERE...

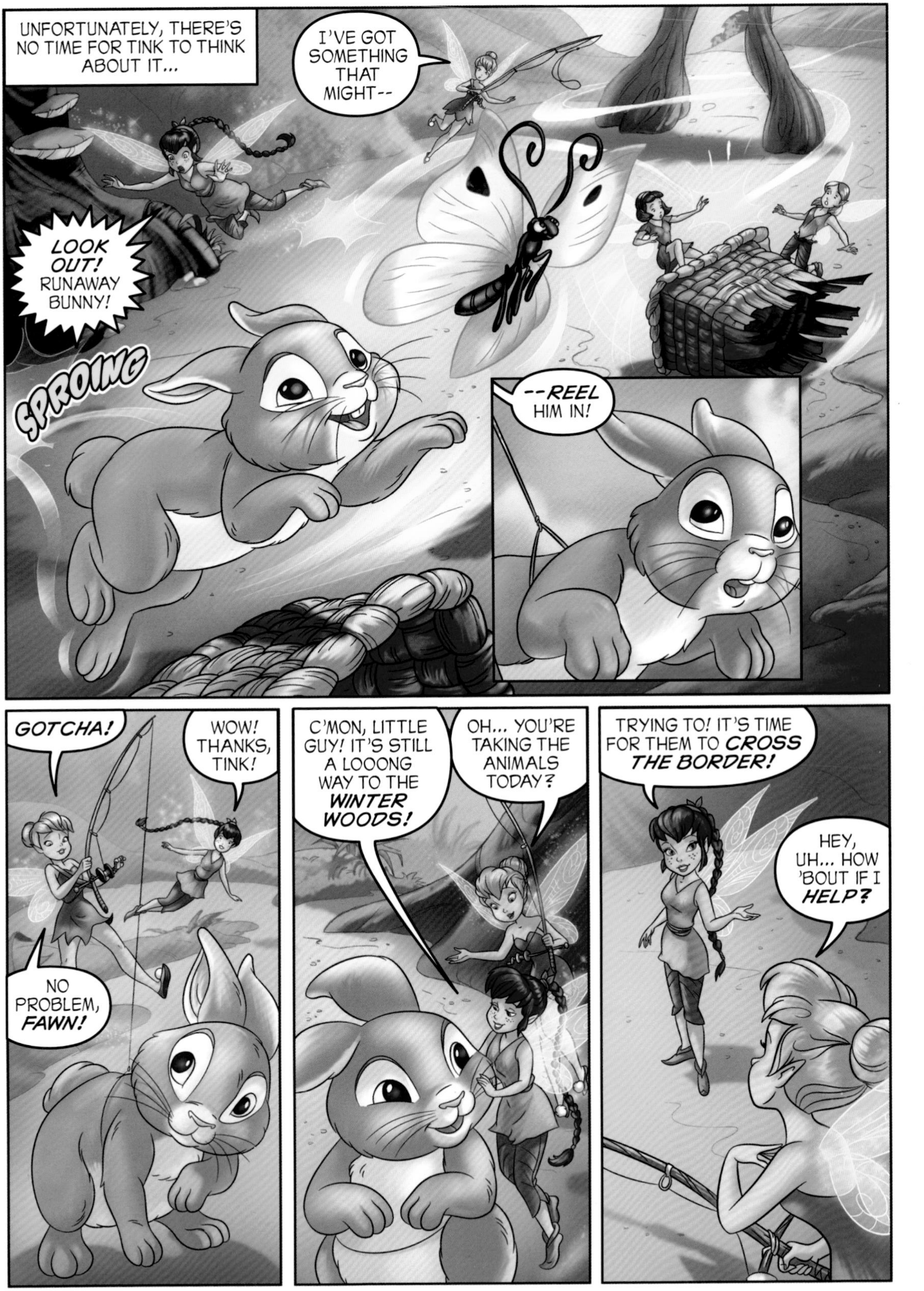
UNFORTUNATELY, THERE'S NO TIME FOR TINK TO THINK ABOUT IT...
I'VE GOT SOMETHING THAT MIGHT--
LOOK OUT! RUNAWAY BUNNY!
SPROING
--REEL HIM IN!
GOTCHA!
WOW! THANKS, TINK!
NO PROBLEM, FAWN!
C'MON, LITTLE GUY! IT'S STILL A LOOONG WAY TO THE WINTER WOODS!
OH... YOU'RE TAKING THE ANIMALS TODAY?
TRYING TO! IT'S TIME FOR THEM TO CROSS THE BORDER!
HEY, UH... HOW 'BOUT IF I HELP?

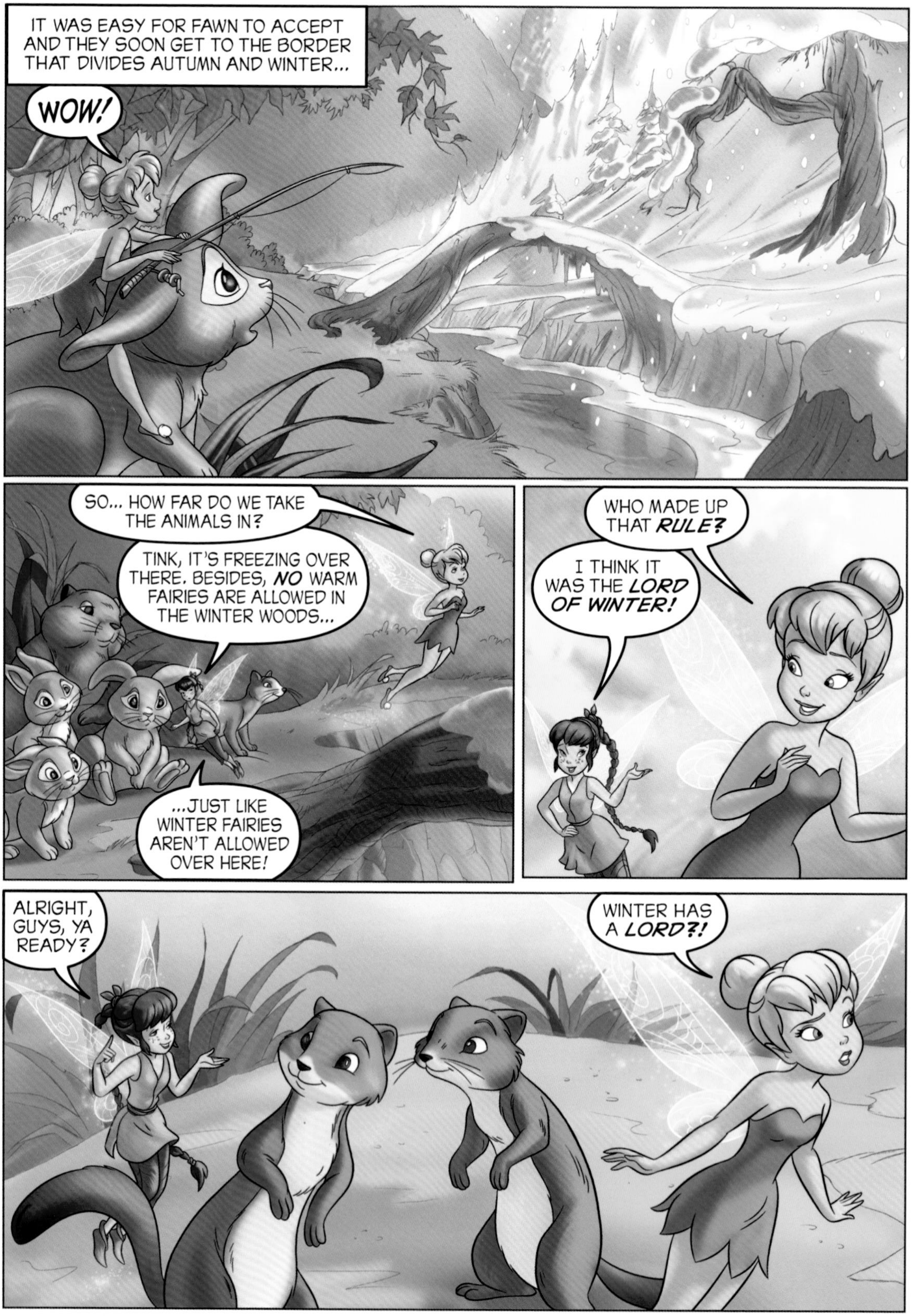
IT WAS EASY FOR FAWN TO ACCEPT AND THEY SOON GET TO THE BORDER THAT DIVIDES AUTUMN AND WINTER...
WOW!
SO... HOW FAR DO WE TAKE THE ANIMALS IN?
TINK, IT'S FREEZING OVER THERE. BESIDES, NO WARM FAIRIES ARE ALLOWED IN THE WINTER WOODS...
...JUST LIKE WINTER FAIRIES AREN'T ALLOWED OVER HERE!
WHO MADE UP THAT RULE?
I THINK IT WAS THE LORD OF WINTER!
ALRIGHT, GUYS, YA READY?
WINTER HAS A LORD?!

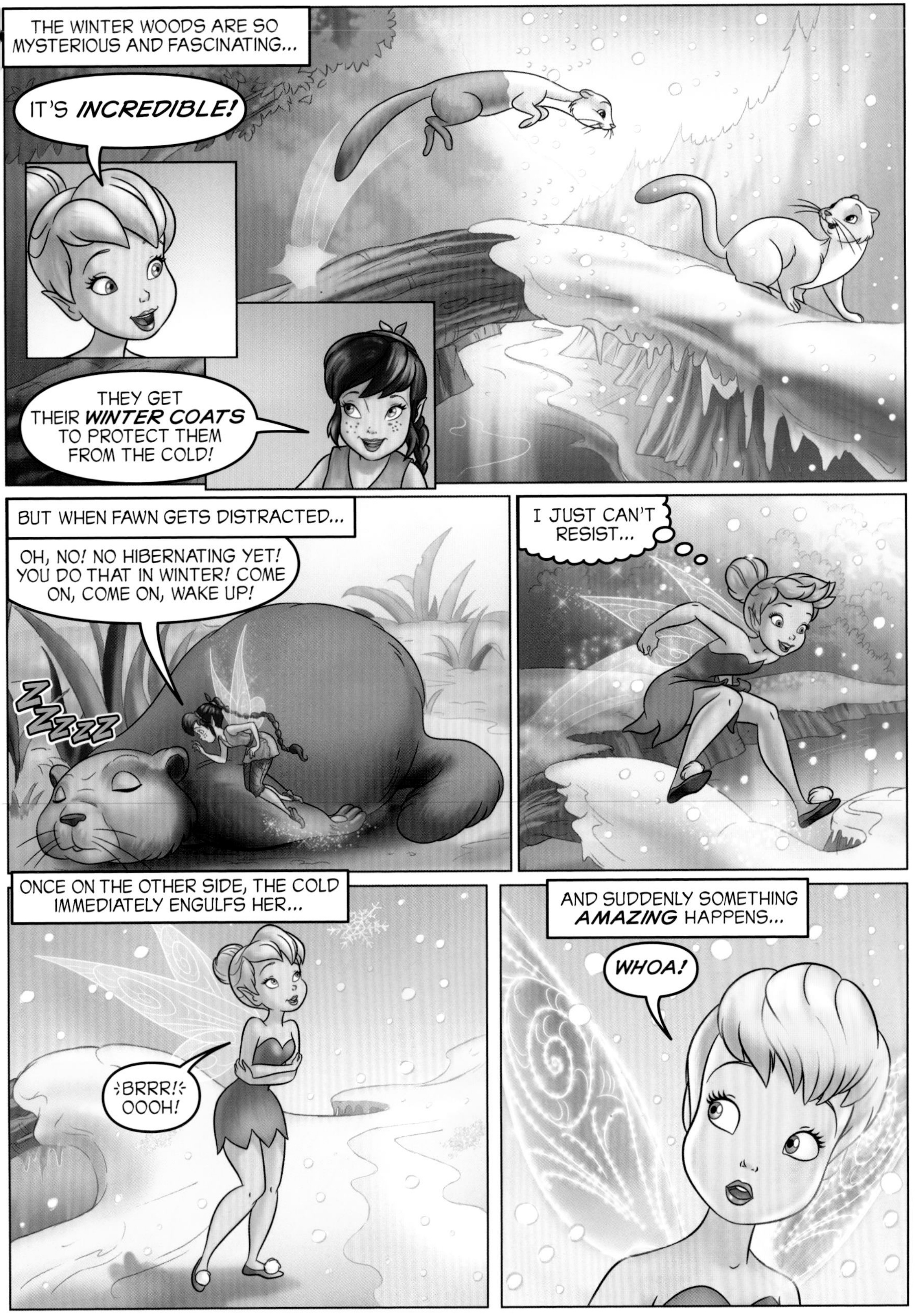
THE WINTER WOODS ARE SO MYSTERIOUS AND FASCINATING...
IT'S INCREDIBLE!
THEY GET THEIR WINTER COATS TO PROTECT THEM FROM THE COLD!
BUT WHEN FAWN GETS DISTRACTED...
OH, NO! NO HIBERNATING YET! YOU DO THAT IN WINTER! COME ON, COME ON, WAKE UP!
ZZZZZ
I JUST CAN'T RESIST...
ONCE ON THE OTHER SIDE, THE COLD IMMEDIATELY ENGULFS HER...
BRRR! OOOH!
AND SUDDENLY SOMETHING AMAZING HAPPENS...
WHOA!

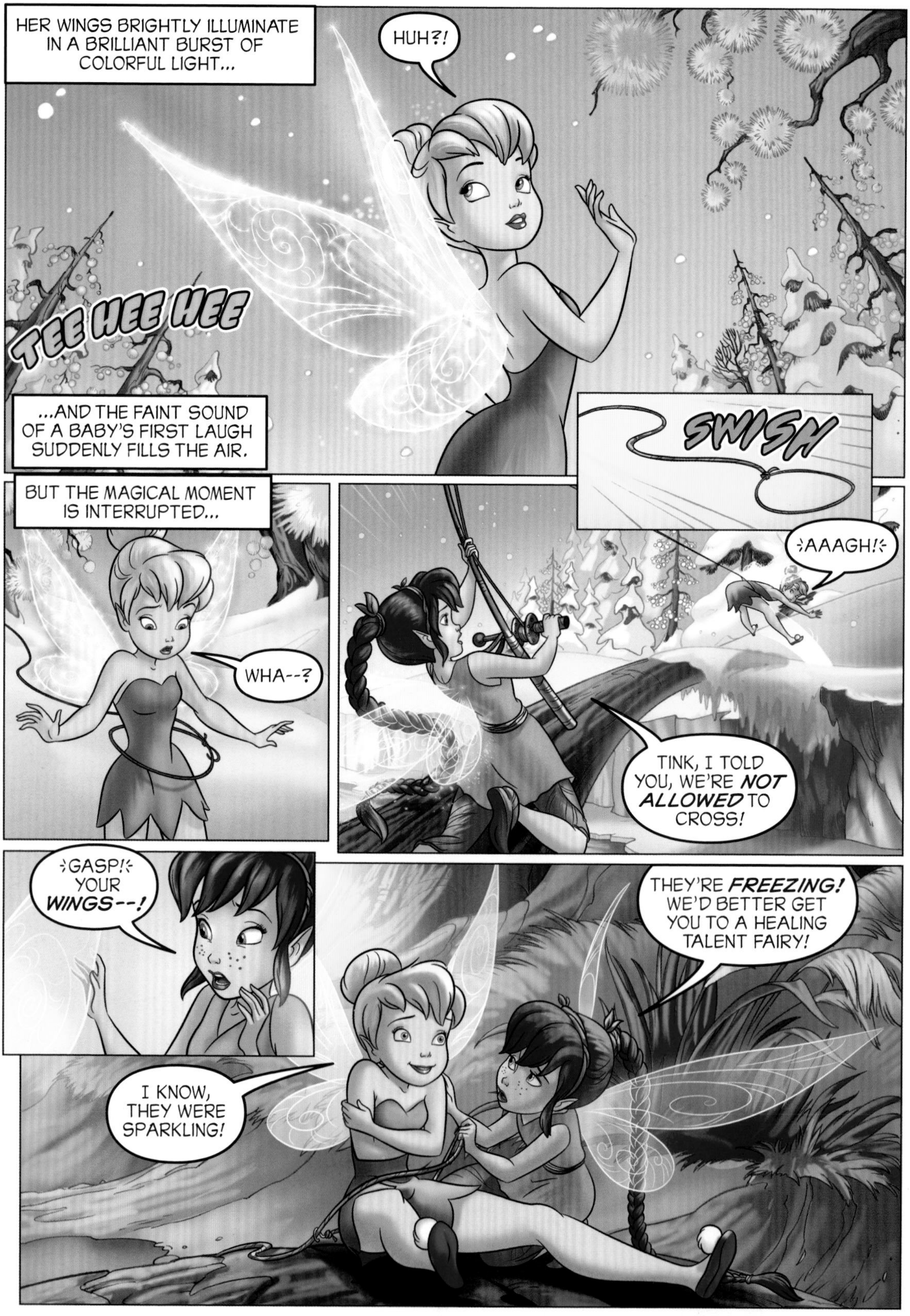
HER WINGS BRIGHTLY ILLUMINATE IN A BRILLIANT BURST OF COLORFUL LIGHT...
HUH?!
TEE HEE HEE
...AND THE FAINT SOUND OF A BABY'S FIRST LAUGH SUDDENLY FILLS THE AIR.
SWISH
BUT THE MAGICAL MOMENT IS INTERRUPTED...
WHA--?
AAAGH!
TINK, I TOLD YOU, WE'RE NOT ALLOWED TO CROSS!
GASP! YOUR WINGS--!
THEY'RE FREEZING! WE'D BETTER GET YOU TO A HEALING TALENT FAIRY!
I KNOW, THEY WERE SPARKLING!

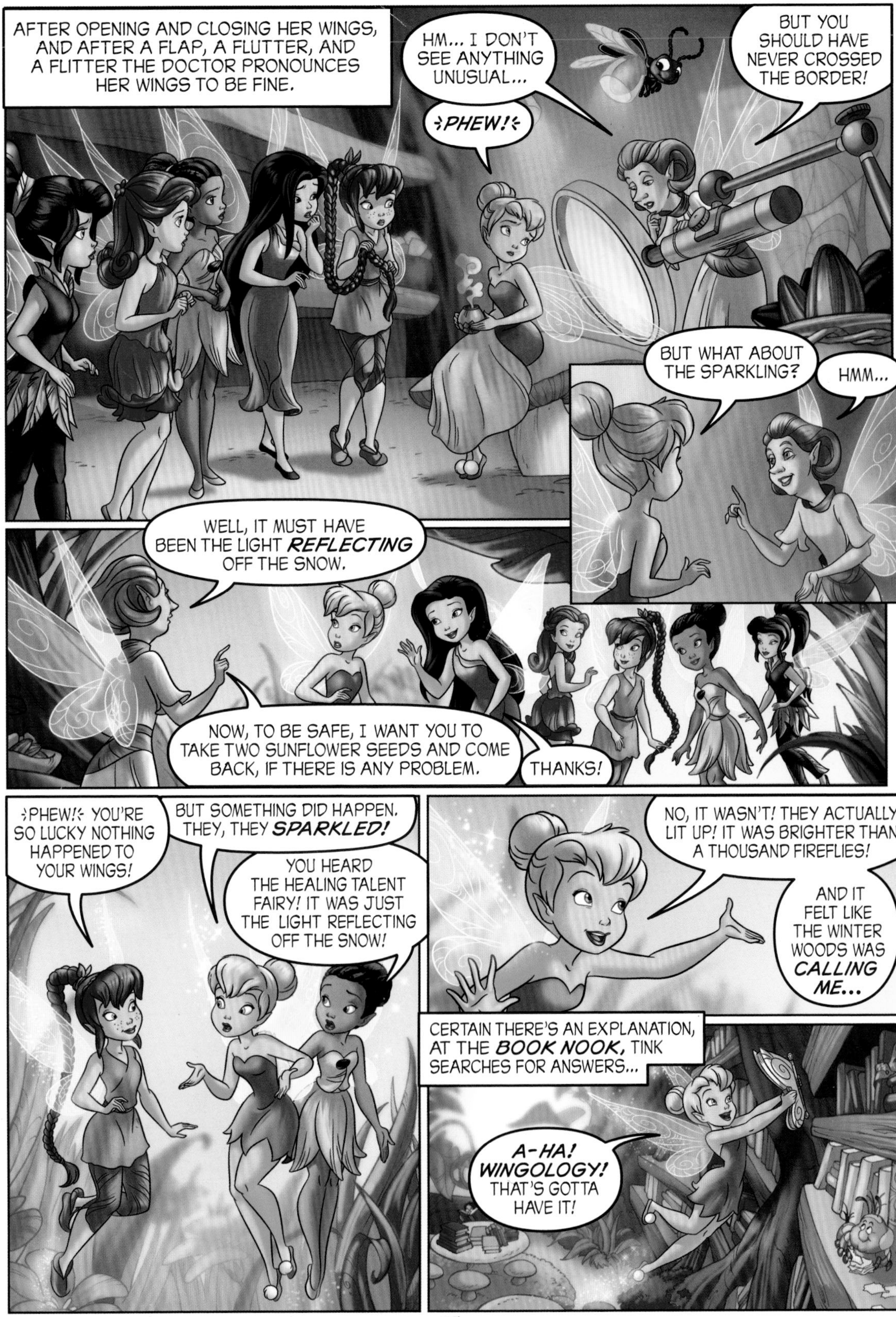
AFTER OPENING AND CLOSING HER WINGS, AND AFTER A FLAP, A FLUTTER, AND A FLITTER THE DOCTOR PRONOUNCES HER WINGS TO BE FINE.
HM... I DON'T SEE ANYTHING UNUSUAL...
PHEW!
BUT YOU SHOULD HAVE NEVER CROSSED THE BORDER!
BUT WHAT ABOUT THE SPARKLING?
HMM...
WELL, IT MUST HAVE BEEN THE LIGHT REFLECTING OFF THE SNOW.
NOW, TO BE SAFE, I WANT YOU TO TAKE TWO SUNFLOWER SEEDS AND COME BACK, IF THERE IS ANY PROBLEM.
THANKS!
PHEW! YOU'RE SO LUCKY NOTHING HAPPENED TO YOUR WINGS!
BUT SOMETHING DID HAPPEN. THEY, THEY SPARKLED!
YOU HEARD THE HEALING TALENT FAIRY! IT WAS JUST THE LIGHT REFLECTING OFF THE SNOW!
NO, IT WASN'T! THEY ACTUALLY LIT UP! IT WAS BRIGHTER THAN A THOUSAND FIREFLIES!
AND IT FELT LIKE THE WINTER WOODS WAS CALLING ME...
CERTAIN THERE'S AN EXPLANATION, AT THE BOOK NOOK, TINK SEARCHES FOR ANSWERS...
A-HA! WINGOLOGY! THAT'S GOTTA HAVE IT!

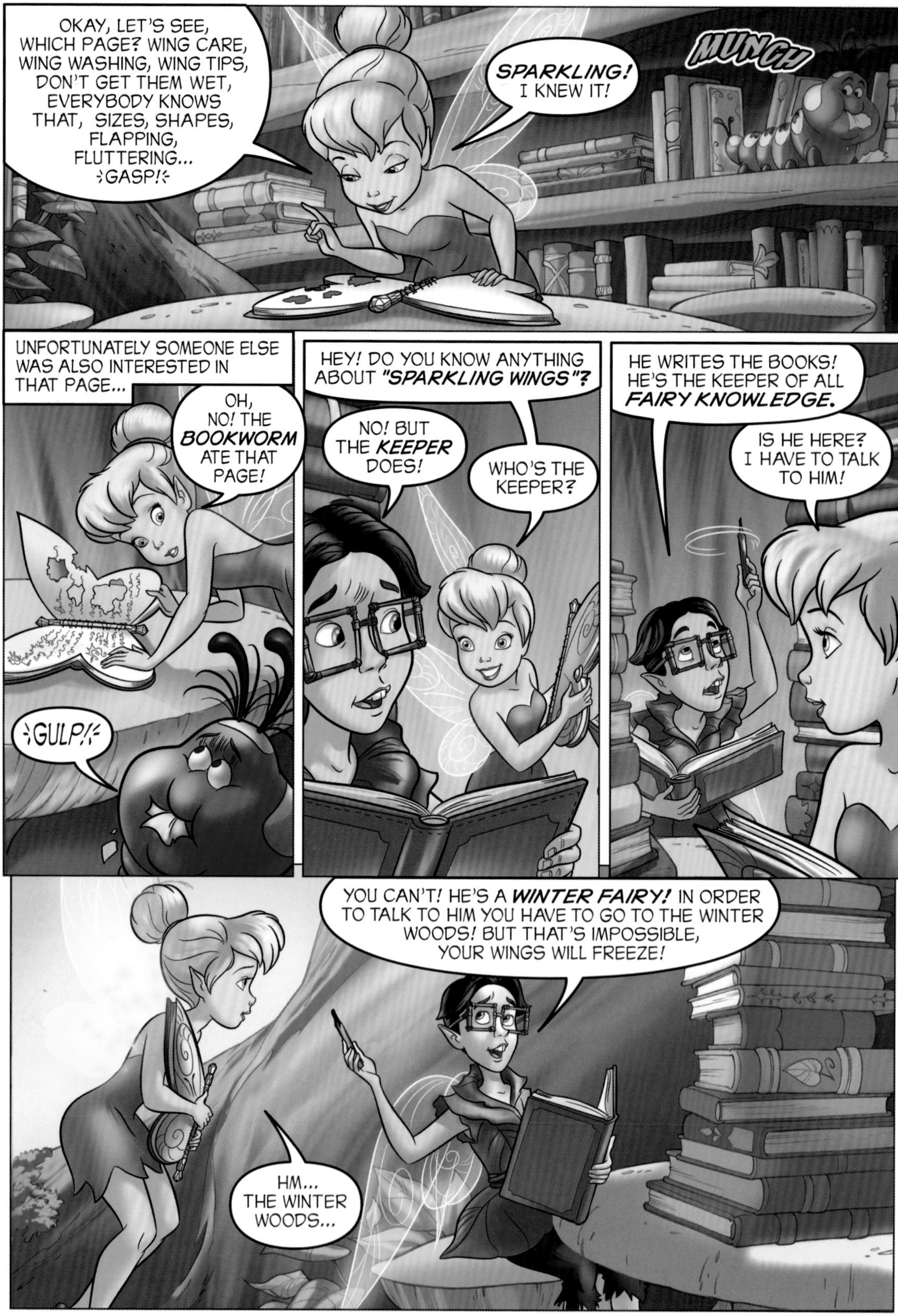
OKAY, LET'S SEE, WHICH PAGE? WING CARE, WING WASHING, WING TIPS, DON'T GET THEM WET, EVERYBODY KNOWS THAT, SIZES, SHAPES, FLAPPING, FLUTTERING... GASP!
SPARKLING! I KNEW IT!
MUNCH
UNFORTUNATELY SOMEONE ELSE WAS ALSO INTERESTED IN THAT PAGE...
OH, NO! THE BOOKWORM ATE THAT PAGE!
GULP!
HEY! DO YOU KNOW ANYTHING ABOUT "SPARKLING WINGS"?
NO! BUT THE KEEPER DOES!
WHO'S THE KEEPER?
HE WRITES THE BOOKS! HE'S THE KEEPER OF ALL FAIRY KNOWLEDGE.
IS HE HERE? I HAVE TO TALK TO HIM!
YOU CAN'T! HE'S A WINTER FAIRY! IN ORDER TO TALK TO HIM YOU HAVE TO GO TO THE WINTER WOODS! BUT THAT'S IMPOSSIBLE, YOUR WINGS WILL FREEZE!
HM... THE WINTER WOODS...

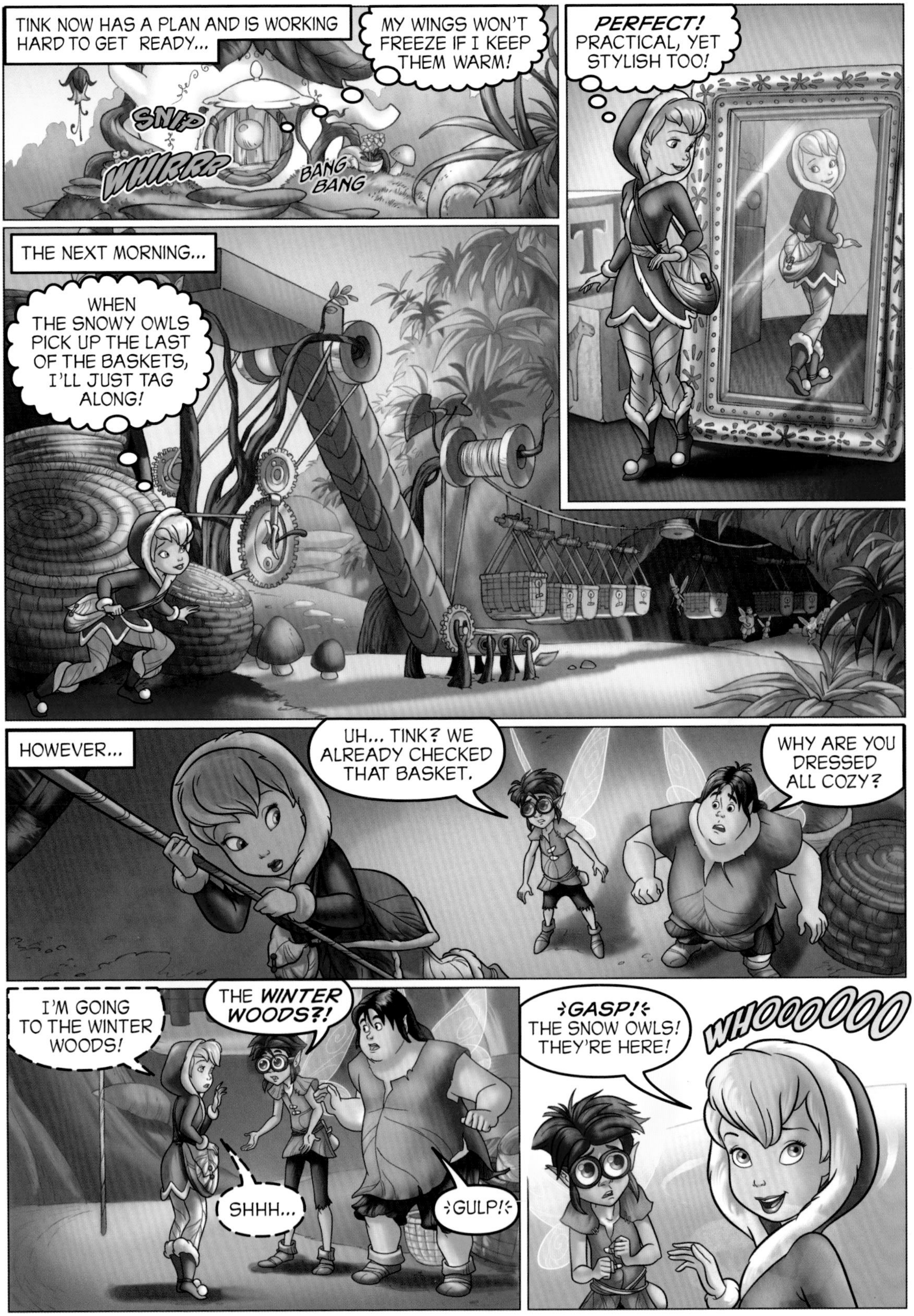

TINK NOW HAS A PLAN AND IS WORKING HARD TO GET READY...
MY WINGS WON'T FREEZE IF I KEEP THEM WARM!
SNIP
WHIRRR
BANG BANG
PERFECT! PRACTICAL, YET STYLISH TOO!
THE NEXT MORNING...
WHEN THE SNOWY OWLS PICK UP THE LAST OF THE BASKETS, I'LL JUST TAG ALONG!
HOWEVER...
UH... TINK? WE ALREADY CHECKED THAT BASKET.
WHY ARE YOU DRESSED ALL COZY?
I'M GOING TO THE WINTER WOODS!
THE WINTER WOODS?!
SHHH...
GULP!
GASP! THE SNOW OWLS! THEY'RE HERE!
WHOOOOOO

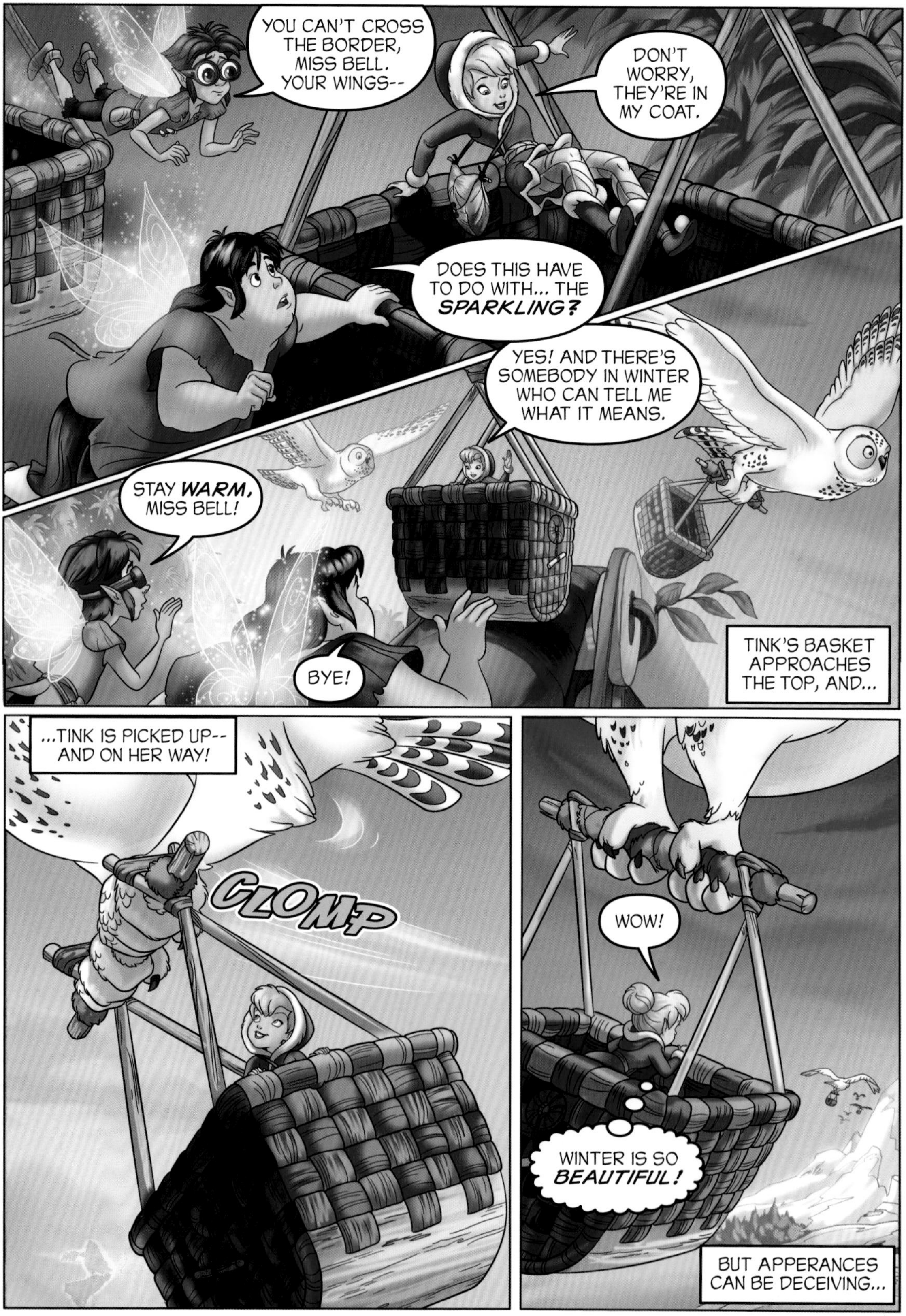
YOU CAN'T CROSS THE BORDER, MISS BELL. YOUR WINGS--
DON'T WORRY, THEY'RE IN MY COAT.
DOES THIS HAVE TO DO WITH... THE *SPARKLING?*
YES! AND THERE'S SOMEBODY IN WINTER WHO CAN TELL ME WHAT IT MEANS.
STAY **WARM,** MISS BELL!
BYE!
TINK'S BASKET APPROACHES THE TOP, AND...
...TINK IS PICKED UP-- AND ON HER WAY!
CLOMP
WOW!
WINTER IS SO **BEAUTIFUL!**
BUT APPERANCES CAN BE DECEIVING...

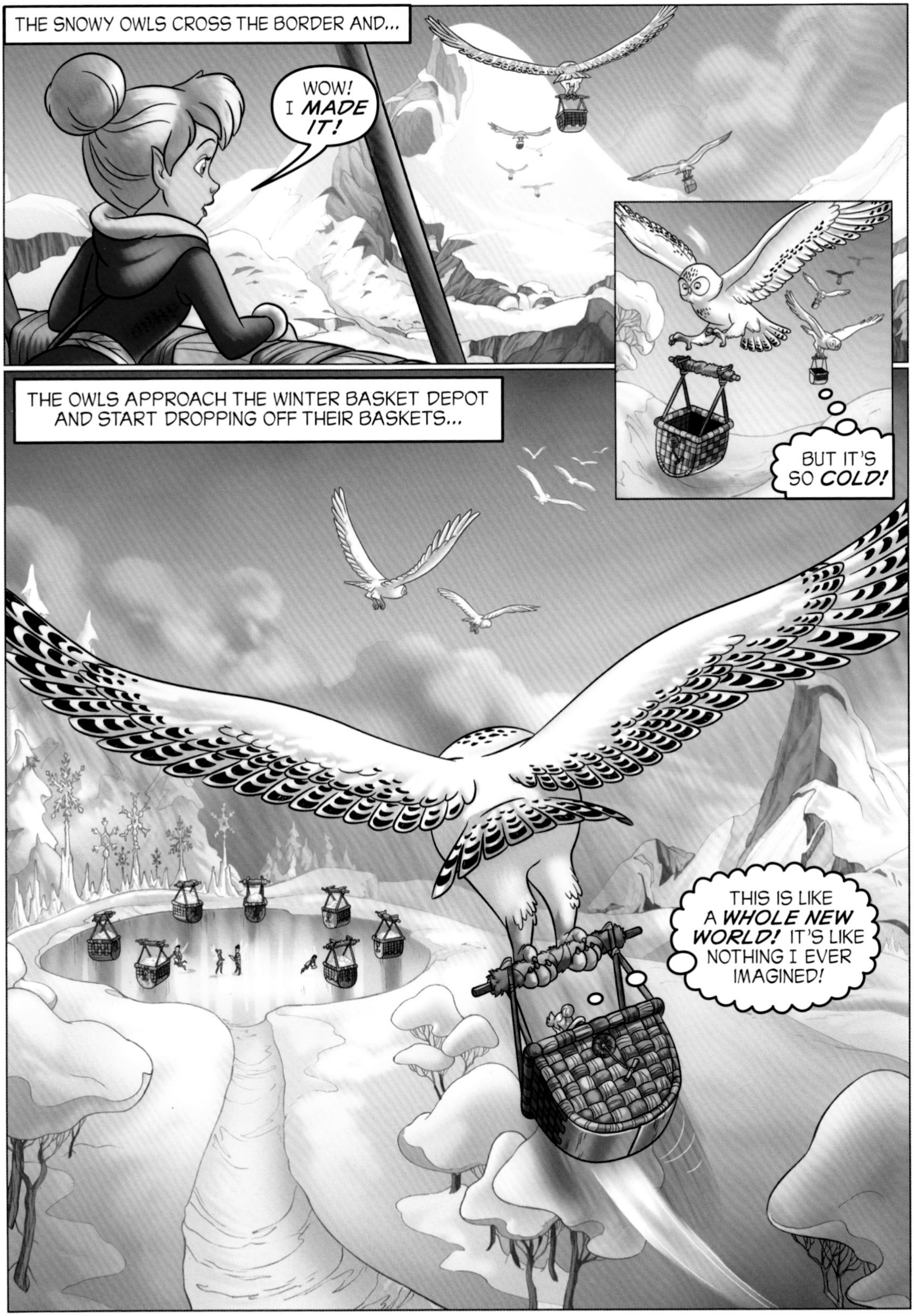
THE SNOWY OWLS CROSS THE BORDER AND...
WOW! I *MADE IT!*
BUT IT'S SO *COLD!*
THE OWLS APPROACH THE WINTER BASKET DEPOT AND START DROPPING OFF THEIR BASKETS...
THIS IS LIKE A *WHOLE NEW WORLD!* IT'S LIKE NOTHING I EVER IMAGINED!

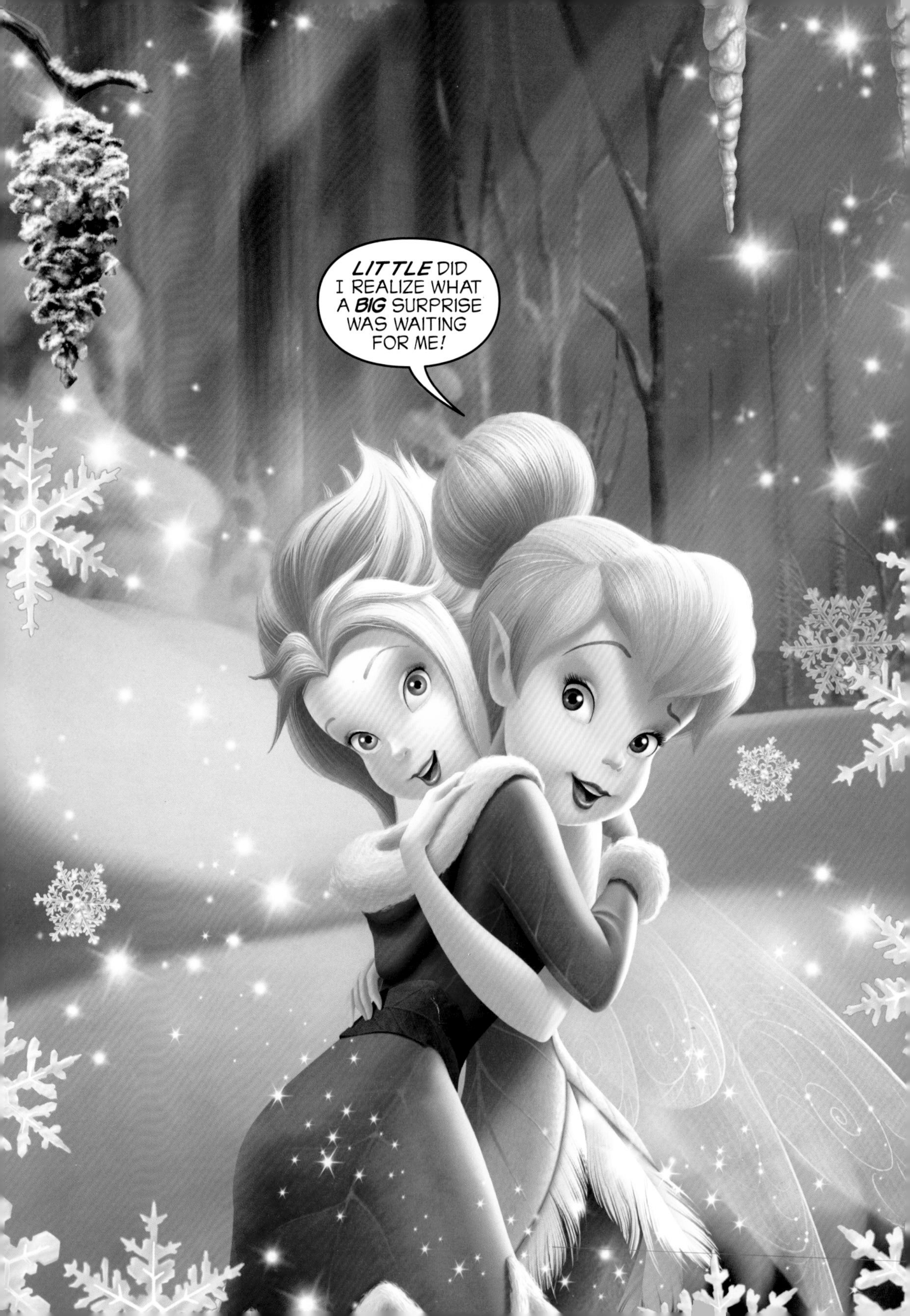
LITTLE DID I REALIZE WHAT A BIG SURPRISE WAS WAITING FOR ME!

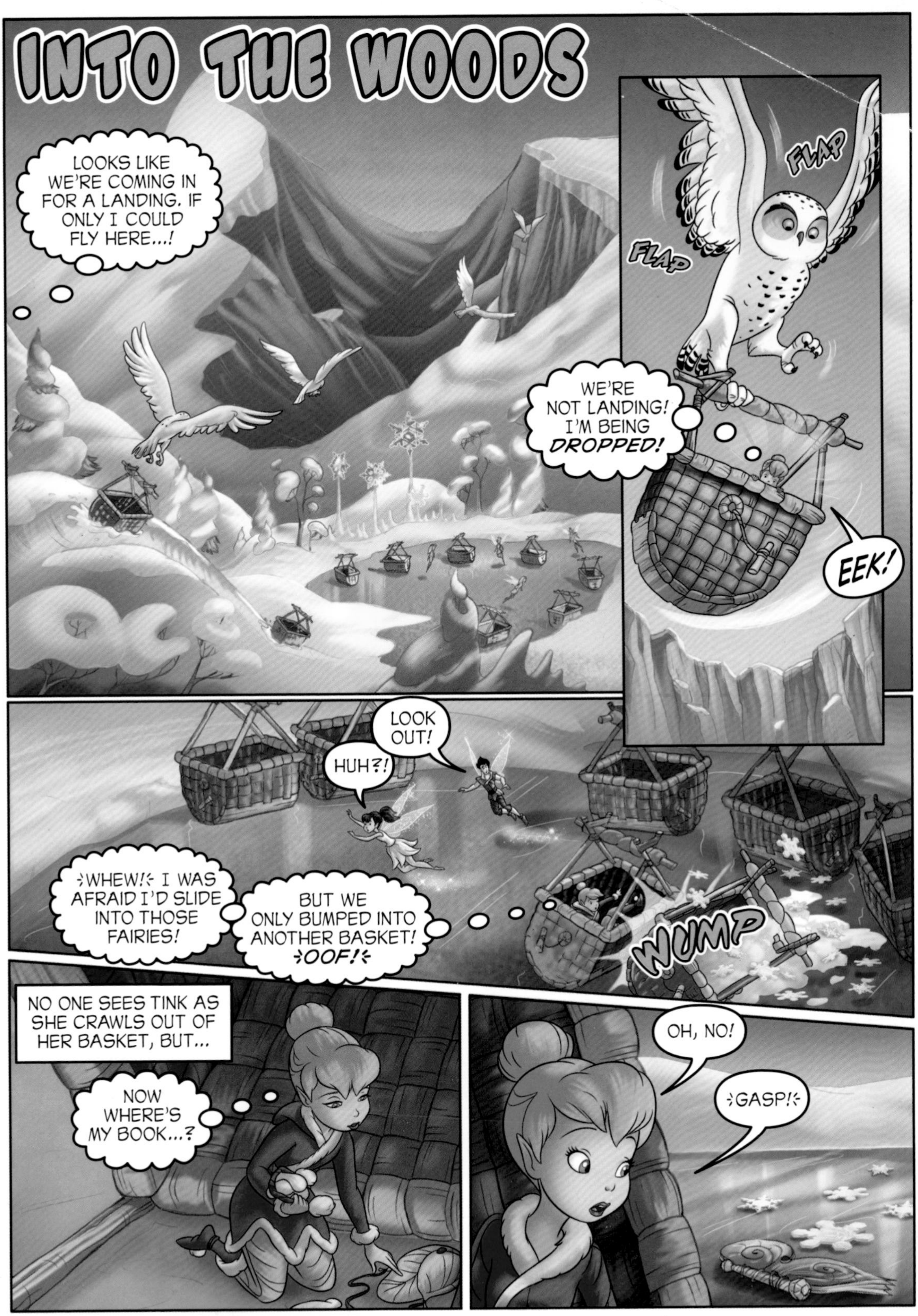
INTO THE WOODS
LOOKS LIKE WE'RE COMING IN FOR A LANDING. IF ONLY I COULD FLY HERE...!
FLAP
FLAP
WE'RE NOT LANDING! I'M BEING DROPPED!
EEK!
LOOK OUT!
HUH?!
WHEW! I WAS AFRAID I'D SLIDE INTO THOSE FAIRIES!
BUT WE ONLY BUMPED INTO ANOTHER BASKET! OOF!
WUMP
NO ONE SEES TINK AS SHE CRAWLS OUT OF HER BASKET, BUT...
NOW WHERE'S MY BOOK...?
OH, NO!
GASP!

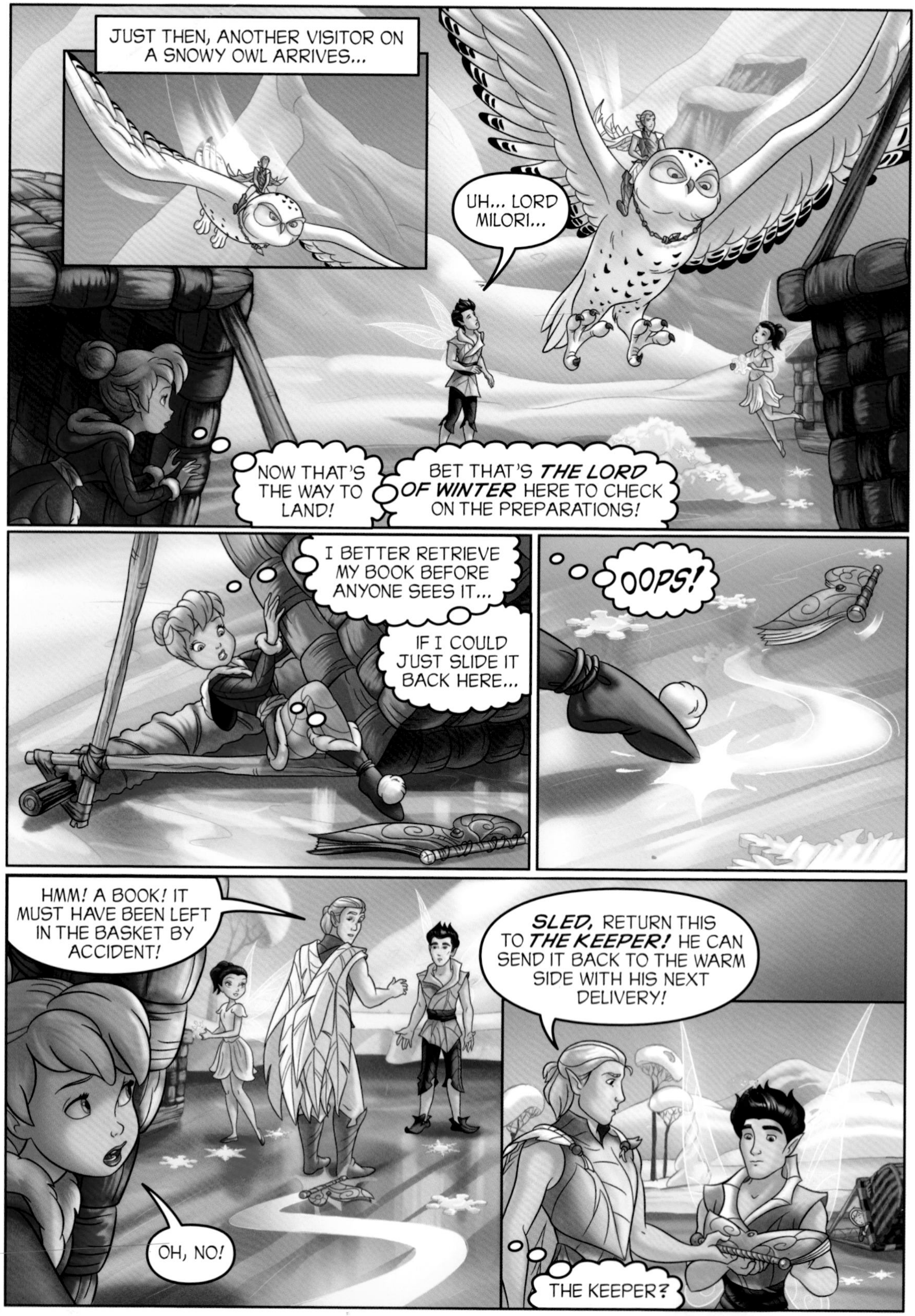
JUST THEN, ANOTHER VISITOR ON A SNOWY OWL ARRIVES...
UH... LORD MILORI...
NOW THAT'S THE WAY TO LAND!
BET THAT'S THE LORD OF WINTER HERE TO CHECK ON THE PREPARATIONS!
I BETTER RETRIEVE MY BOOK BEFORE ANYONE SEES IT...
IF I COULD JUST SLIDE IT BACK HERE...
OOPS!
HMM! A BOOK! IT MUST HAVE BEEN LEFT IN THE BASKET BY ACCIDENT!
OH, NO!
SLED, RETURN THIS TO THE KEEPER! HE CAN SEND IT BACK TO THE WARM SIDE WITH HIS NEXT DELIVERY!
THE KEEPER?

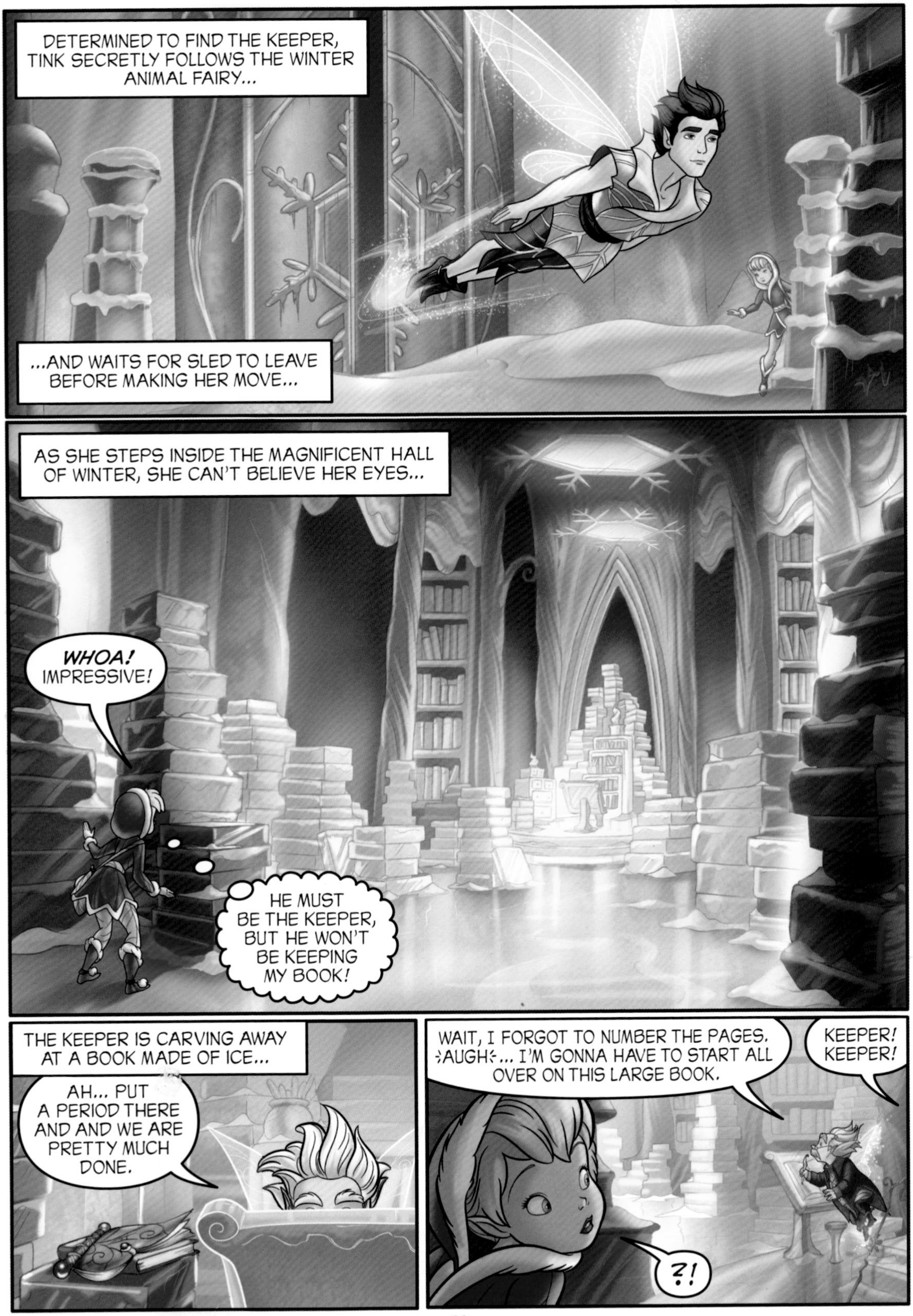
DETERMINED TO FIND THE KEEPER, TINK SECRETLY FOLLOWS THE WINTER ANIMAL FAIRY...
...AND WAITS FOR SLED TO LEAVE BEFORE MAKING HER MOVE...
AS SHE STEPS INSIDE THE MAGNIFICENT HALL OF WINTER, SHE CAN'T BELIEVE HER EYES...
WHOA! IMPRESSIVE!
HE MUST BE THE KEEPER, BUT HE WON'T BE KEEPING MY BOOK!
THE KEEPER IS CARVING AWAY AT A BOOK MADE OF ICE...
AH... PUT A PERIOD THERE AND AND WE ARE PRETTY MUCH DONE.
WAIT, I FORGOT TO NUMBER THE PAGES. AUGH... I'M GONNA HAVE TO START ALL OVER ON THIS LARGE BOOK.
KEEPER! KEEPER!
?!

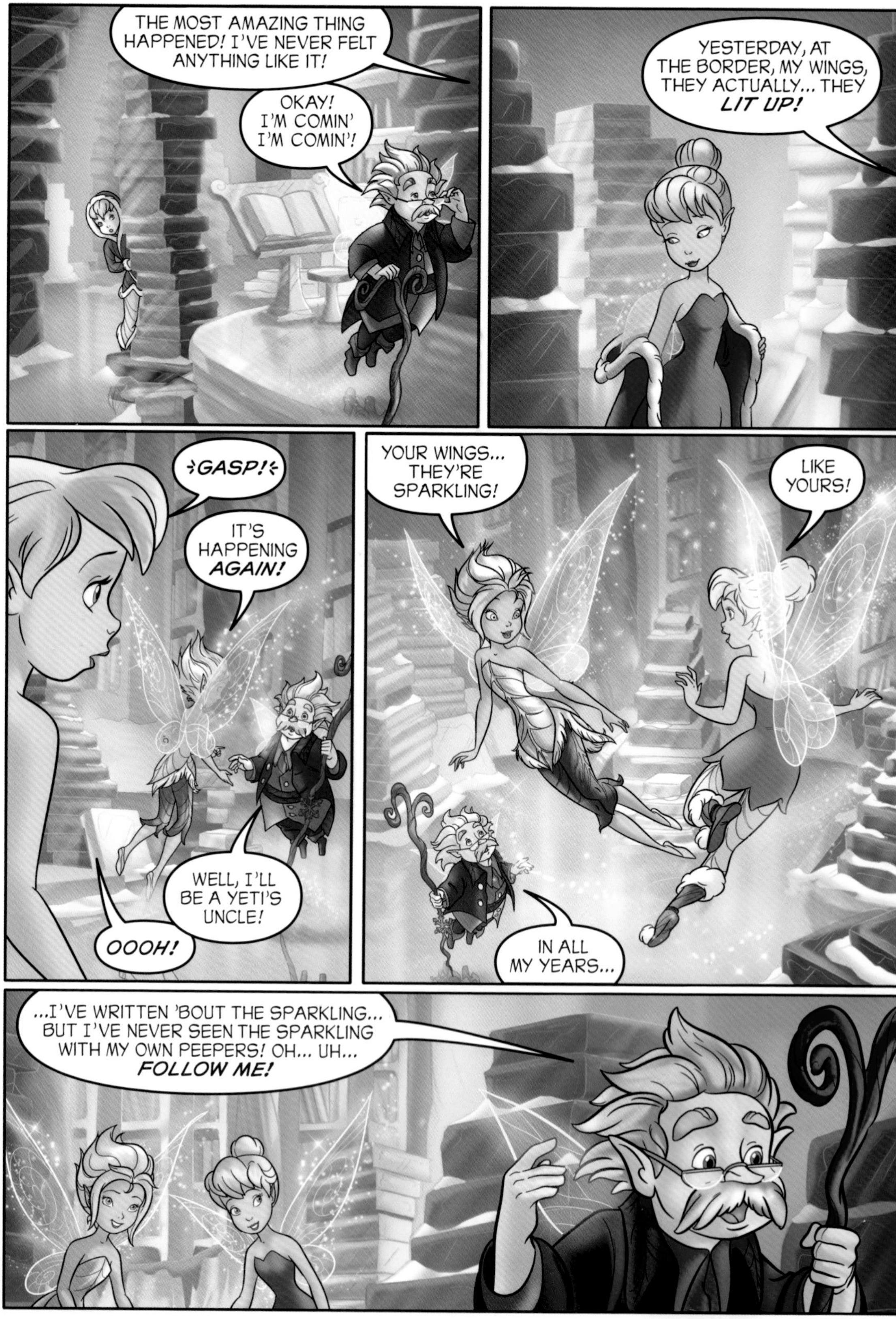

THE MOST AMAZING THING HAPPENED! I'VE NEVER FELT ANYTHING LIKE IT!
OKAY! I'M COMIN' I'M COMIN'!
YESTERDAY, AT THE BORDER, MY WINGS, THEY ACTUALLY... THEY LIT UP!
GASP!
IT'S HAPPENING AGAIN!
WELL, I'LL BE A YETI'S UNCLE!
OOOH!
YOUR WINGS... THEY'RE SPARKLING!
LIKE YOURS!
IN ALL MY YEARS...
...I'VE WRITTEN 'BOUT THE SPARKLING... BUT I'VE NEVER SEEN THE SPARKLING WITH MY OWN PEEPERS! OH... UH... FOLLOW ME!

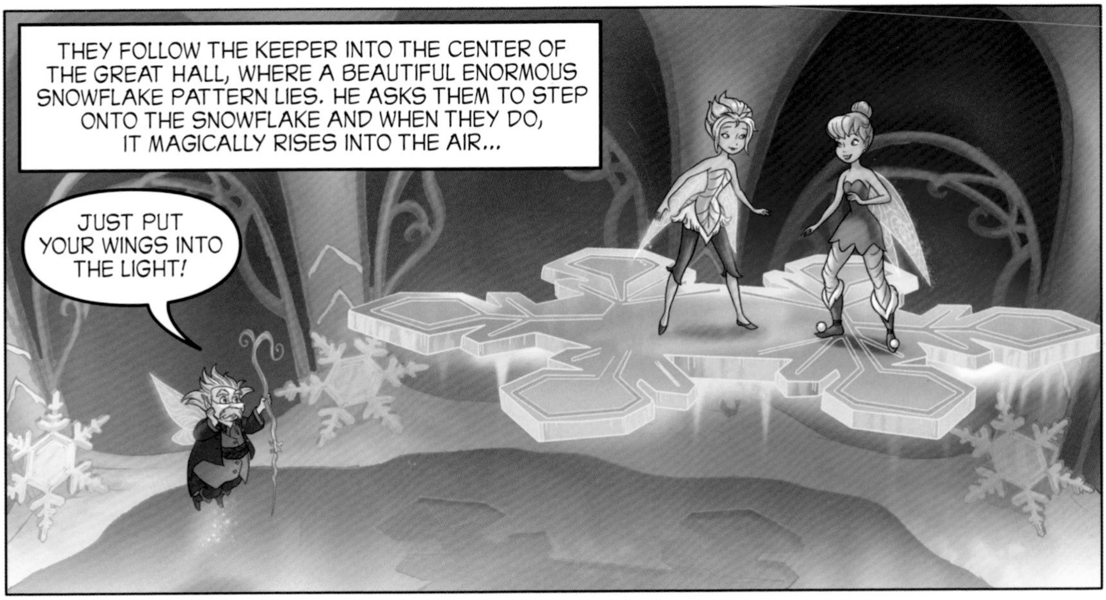
THEY FOLLOW THE KEEPER INTO THE CENTER OF THE GREAT HALL, WHERE A BEAUTIFUL ENORMOUS SNOWFLAKE PATTERN LIES. HE ASKS THEM TO STEP ONTO THE SNOWFLAKE AND WHEN THEY DO, IT MAGICALLY RISES INTO THE AIR...
JUST PUT YOUR WINGS INTO THE LIGHT!

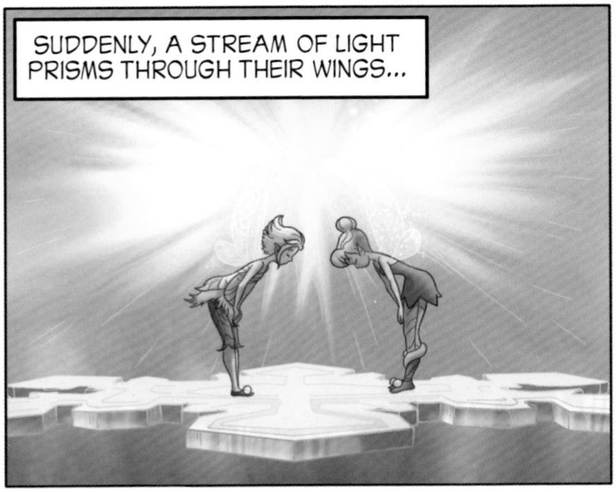
SUDDENLY, A STREAM OF LIGHT PRISMS THROUGH THEIR WINGS...

...PROJECTING IMAGES FROM THEIR PAST ONTO THE ICE CHAMBER WALLS...

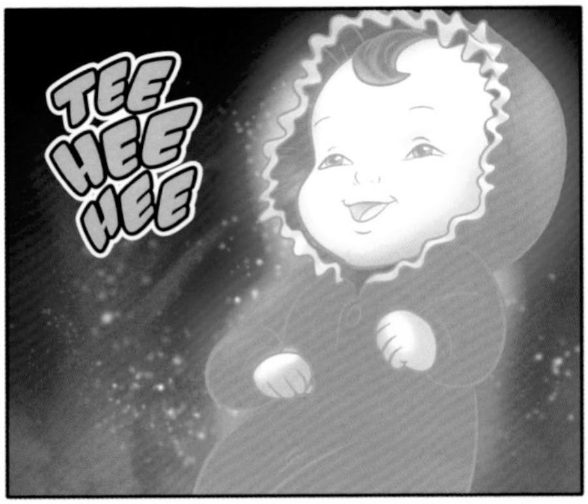
TEE HEE HEE

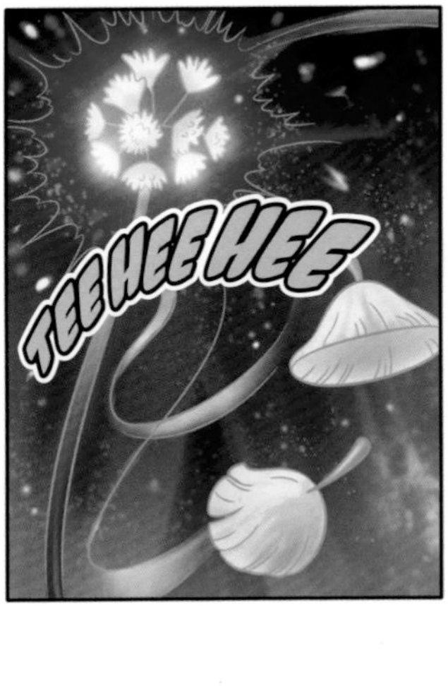
TEE HEE HEE

BOTH WISPS HEAD TOWARD THE PIXIE DUST TREE, BUT ONE GETS CAUGHT IN THE CROOK OF A TREE BRANCH...

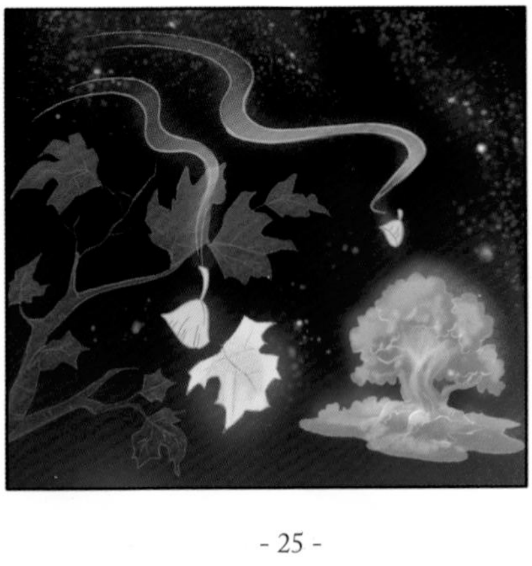

THE WIND SHIFTS, BLOWING THE CAUGHT WISP HARD TOWARD THE WINTER WOODS...

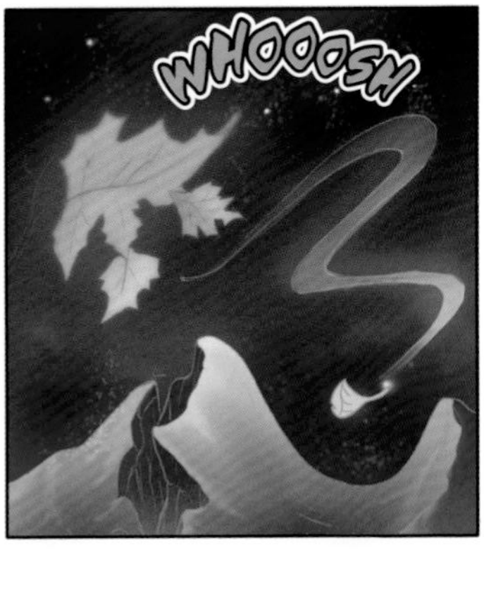
WHOOOSH

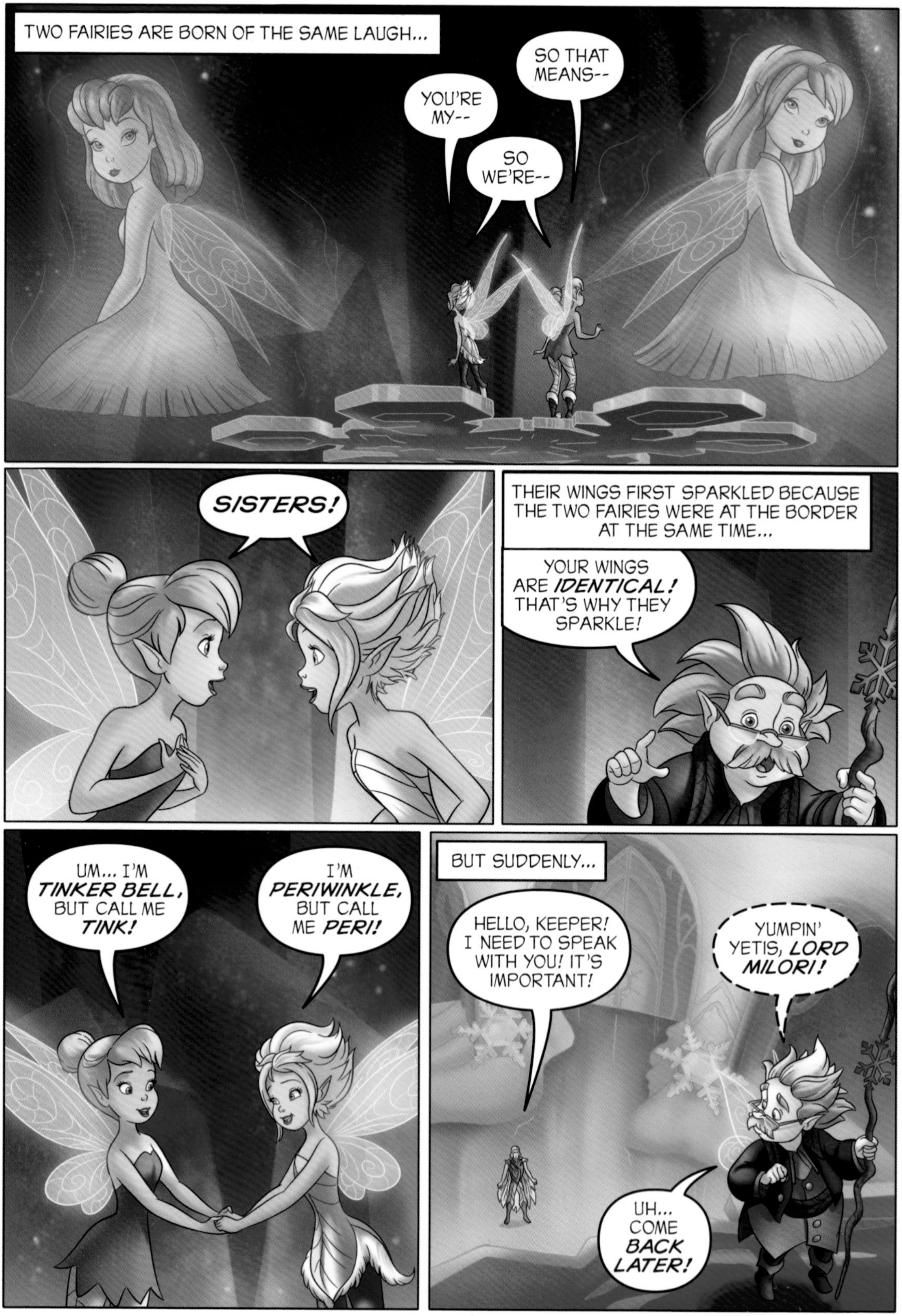

TWO FAIRIES ARE BORN OF THE SAME LAUGH...
YOU'RE MY--
SO THAT MEANS--
SO WE'RE--
SISTERS!
THEIR WINGS FIRST SPARKLED BECAUSE THE TWO FAIRIES WERE AT THE BORDER AT THE SAME TIME...
YOUR WINGS ARE IDENTICAL! THAT'S WHY THEY SPARKLE!
UM... I'M TINKER BELL, BUT CALL ME TINK!
I'M PERIWINKLE, BUT CALL ME PERI!
BUT SUDDENLY...
HELLO, KEEPER! I NEED TO SPEAK WITH YOU! IT'S IMPORTANT!
YUMPIN' YETIS, LORD MILORI!
UH... COME BACK LATER!

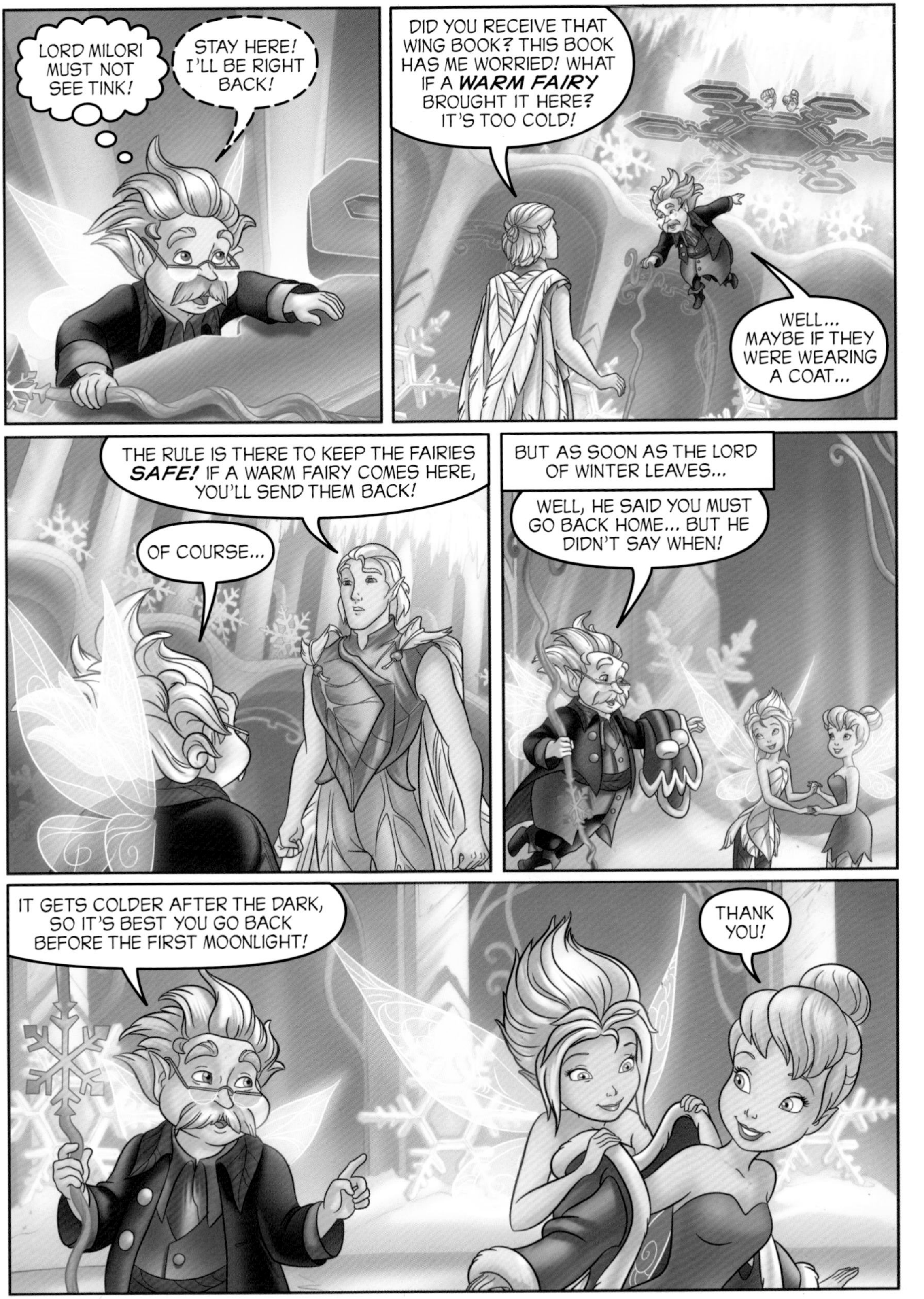
LORD MILORI MUST NOT SEE TINK!
STAY HERE! I'LL BE RIGHT BACK!
DID YOU RECEIVE THAT WING BOOK? THIS BOOK HAS ME WORRIED! WHAT IF A WARM FAIRY BROUGHT IT HERE? IT'S TOO COLD!
WELL... MAYBE IF THEY WERE WEARING A COAT...
THE RULE IS THERE TO KEEP THE FAIRIES SAFE! IF A WARM FAIRY COMES HERE, YOU'LL SEND THEM BACK!
OF COURSE...
BUT AS SOON AS THE LORD OF WINTER LEAVES...
WELL, HE SAID YOU MUST GO BACK HOME... BUT HE DIDN'T SAY WHEN!
IT GETS COLDER AFTER THE DARK, SO IT'S BEST YOU GO BACK BEFORE THE FIRST MOONLIGHT!
THANK YOU!

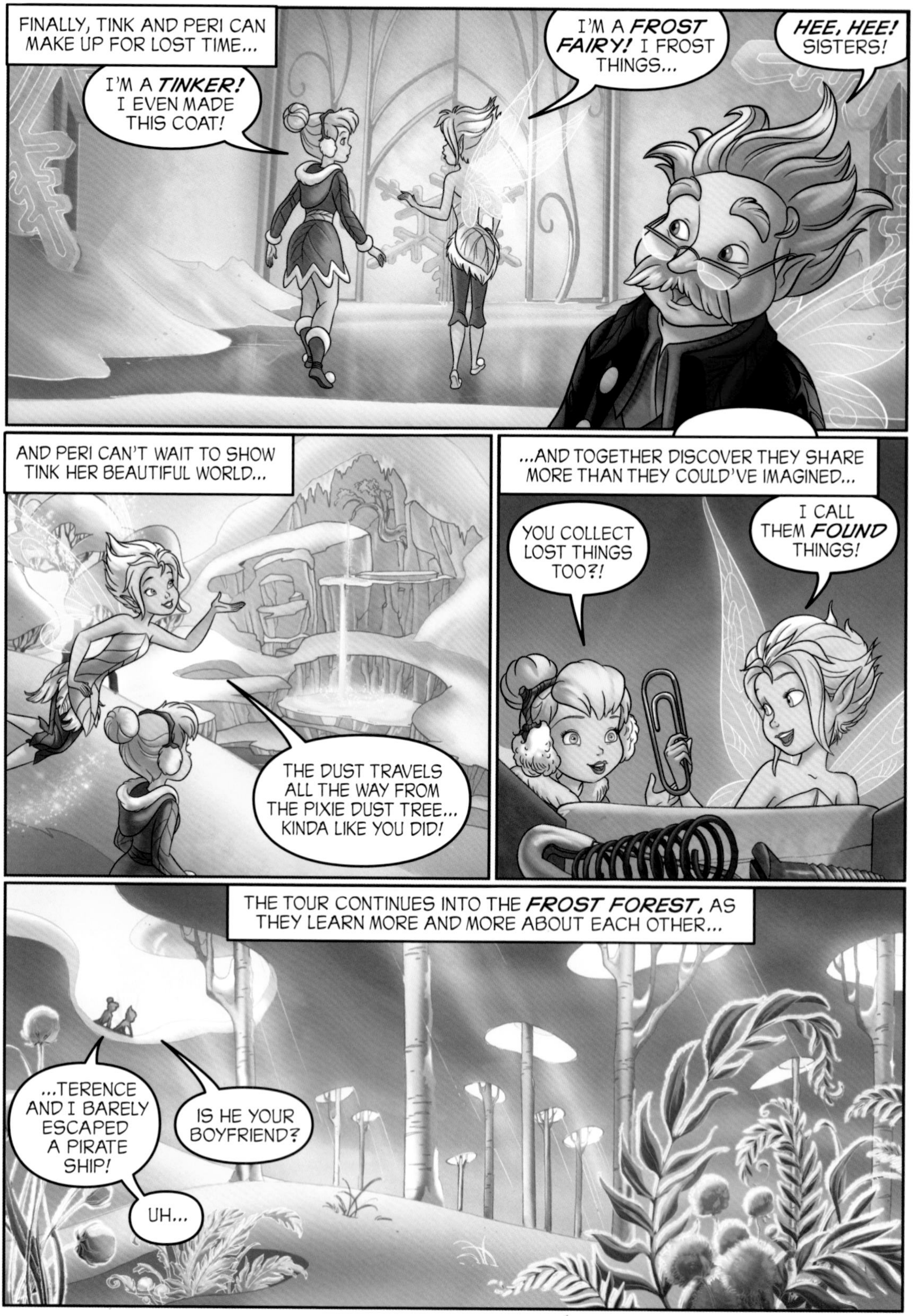
FINALLY, TINK AND PERI CAN MAKE UP FOR LOST TIME...
I'M A *TINKER!* I EVEN MADE THIS COAT!
I'M A *FROST FAIRY!* I FROST THINGS...
HEE, HEE! SISTERS!
AND PERI CAN'T WAIT TO SHOW TINK HER BEAUTIFUL WORLD...
THE DUST TRAVELS ALL THE WAY FROM THE PIXIE DUST TREE... KINDA LIKE YOU DID!
...AND TOGETHER DISCOVER THEY SHARE MORE THAN THEY COULD'VE IMAGINED...
YOU COLLECT LOST THINGS TOO?!
I CALL THEM *FOUND* THINGS!
THE TOUR CONTINUES INTO THE *FROST FOREST,* AS THEY LEARN MORE AND MORE ABOUT EACH OTHER...
...TERENCE AND I BARELY ESCAPED A PIRATE SHIP!
IS HE YOUR BOYFRIEND?
UH...

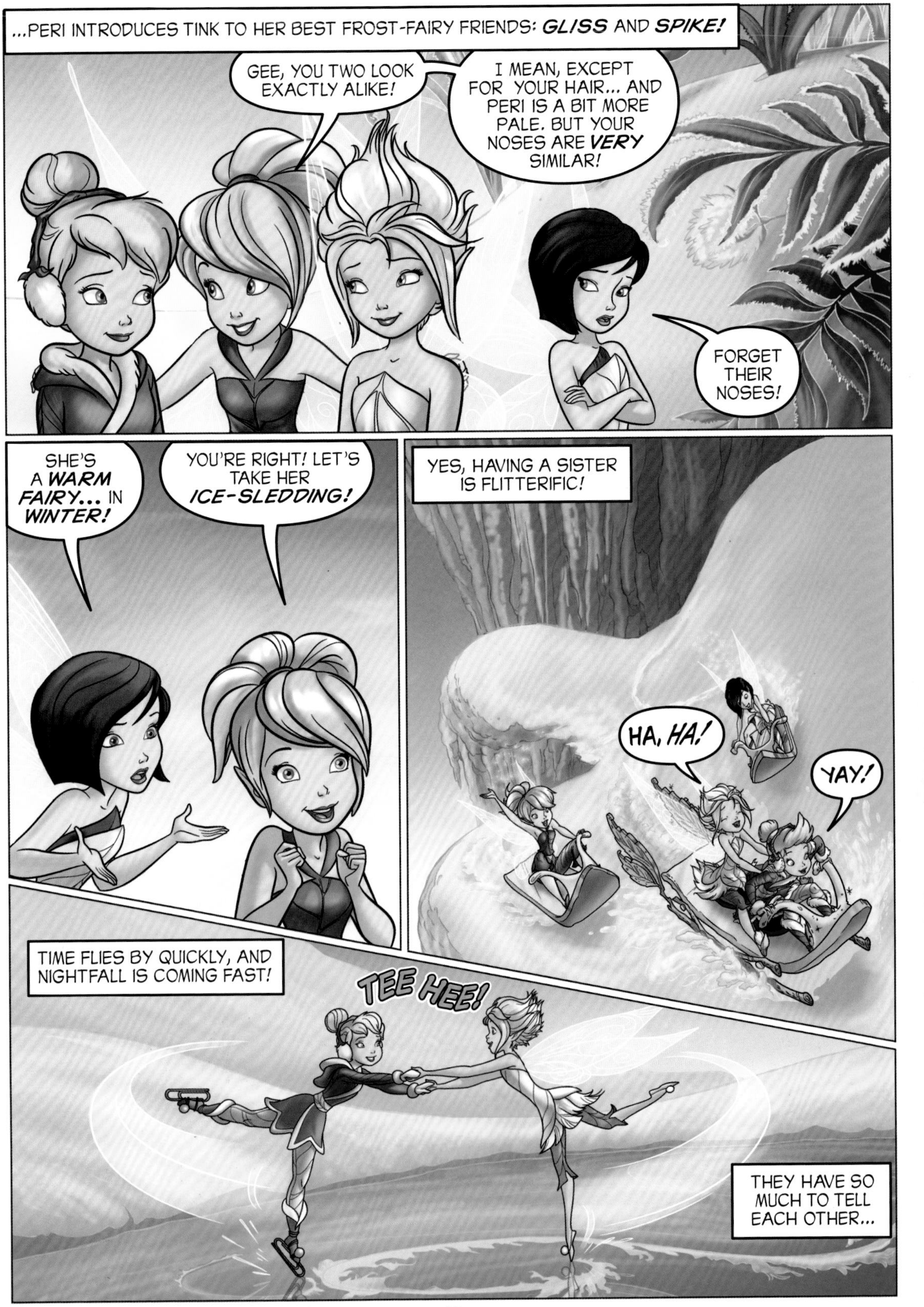
...PERI INTRODUCES TINK TO HER BEST FROST-FAIRY FRIENDS: GLISS AND SPIKE!
GEE, YOU TWO LOOK EXACTLY ALIKE!
I MEAN, EXCEPT FOR YOUR HAIR... AND PERI IS A BIT MORE PALE. BUT YOUR NOSES ARE VERY SIMILAR!
FORGET THEIR NOSES!
SHE'S A WARM FAIRY... IN WINTER!
YOU'RE RIGHT! LET'S TAKE HER ICE-SLEDDING!
YES, HAVING A SISTER IS FLITTERIFIC!
HA, HA!
YAY!
TIME FLIES BY QUICKLY, AND NIGHTFALL IS COMING FAST!
TEE HEE!
THEY HAVE SO MUCH TO TELL EACH OTHER...

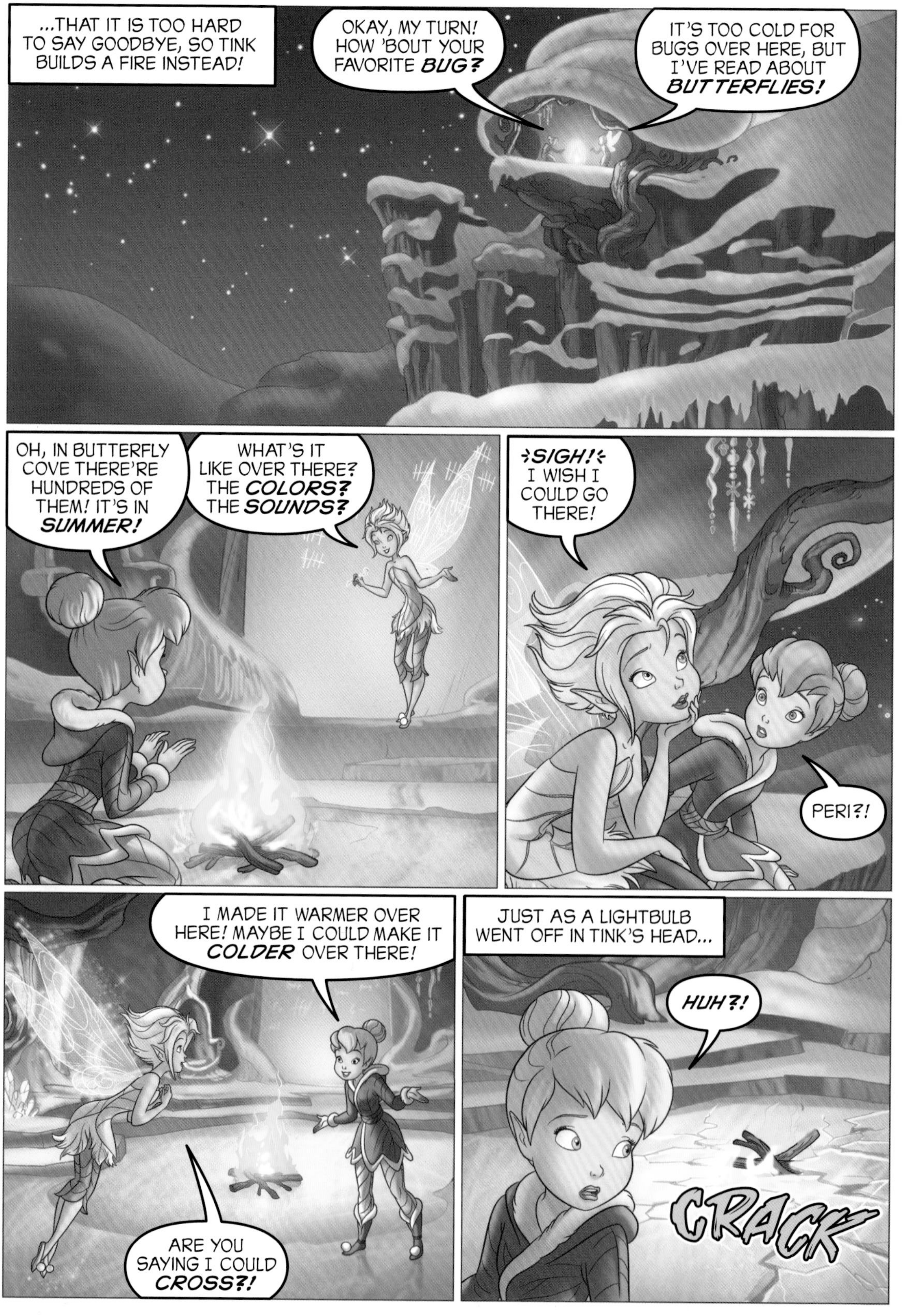
...THAT IT IS TOO HARD TO SAY GOODBYE, SO TINK BUILDS A FIRE INSTEAD!
OKAY, MY TURN! HOW 'BOUT YOUR FAVORITE BUG?
IT'S TOO COLD FOR BUGS OVER HERE, BUT I'VE READ ABOUT BUTTERFLIES!
OH, IN BUTTERFLY COVE THERE'RE HUNDREDS OF THEM! IT'S IN SUMMER!
WHAT'S IT LIKE OVER THERE? THE COLORS? THE SOUNDS?
SIGH! I WISH I COULD GO THERE!
PERI?!
I MADE IT WARMER OVER HERE! MAYBE I COULD MAKE IT COLDER OVER THERE!
ARE YOU SAYING I COULD CROSS?!
JUST AS A LIGHTBULB WENT OFF IN TINK'S HEAD...
HUH?!
CRACK

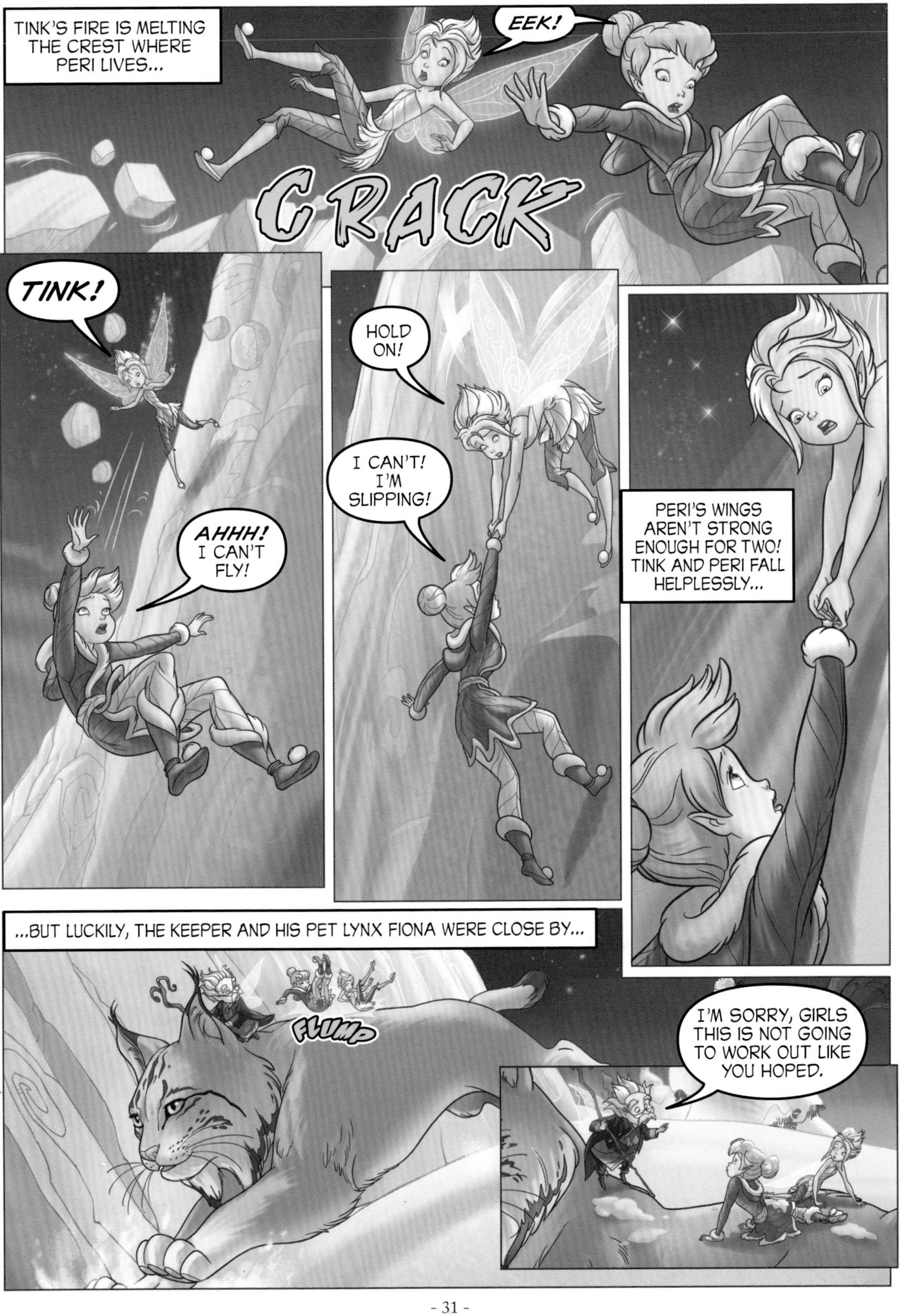

TINK'S FIRE IS MELTING THE CREST WHERE PERI LIVES...
EEK!
CRACK
TINK!
AHHH! I CAN'T FLY!
HOLD ON!
I CAN'T! I'M SLIPPING!
PERI'S WINGS AREN'T STRONG ENOUGH FOR TWO! TINK AND PERI FALL HELPLESSLY...
...BUT LUCKILY, THE KEEPER AND HIS PET LYNX FIONA WERE CLOSE BY...
FLUMP
I'M SORRY, GIRLS THIS IS NOT GOING TO WORK OUT LIKE YOU HOPED.

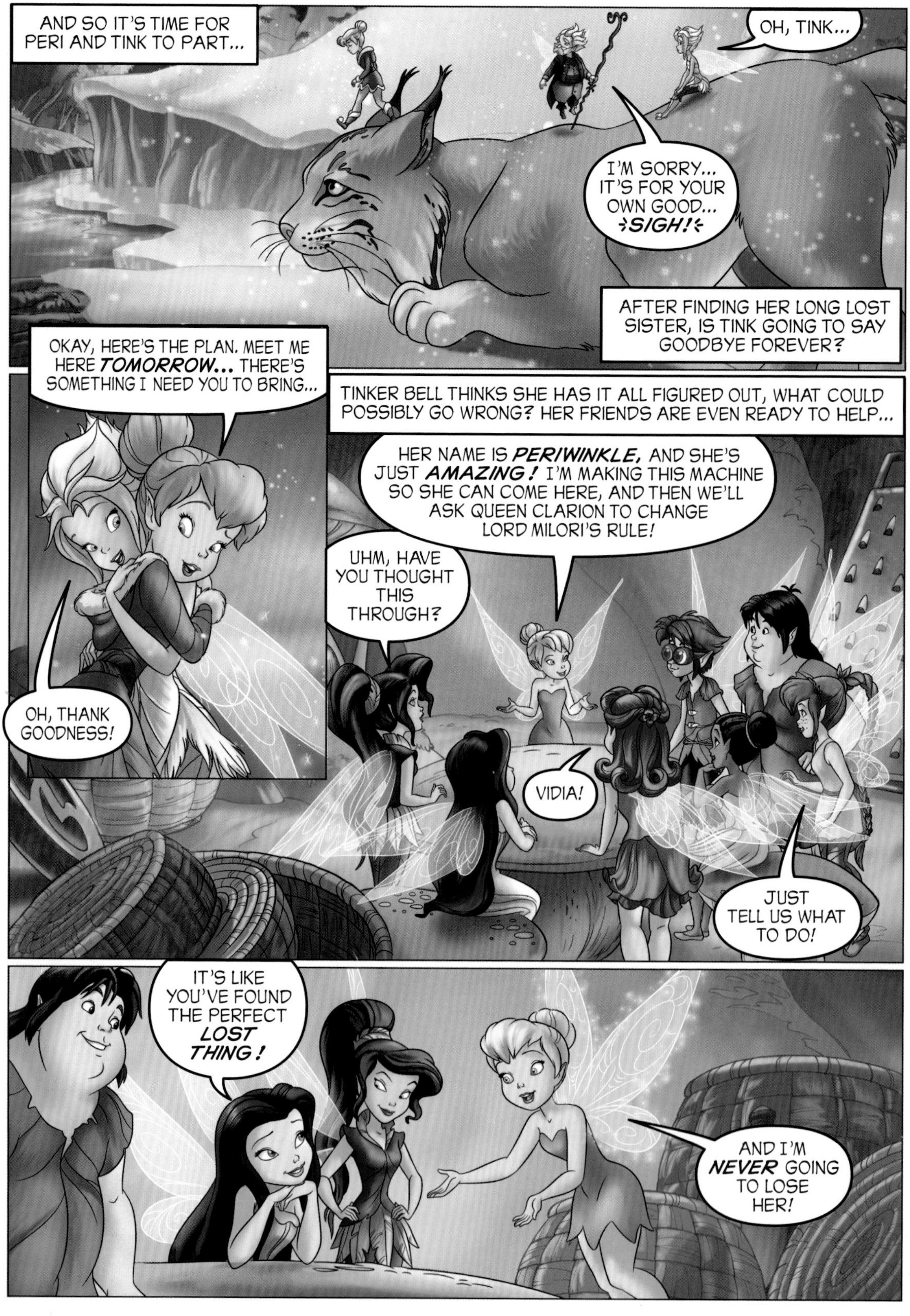
AND SO IT'S TIME FOR PERI AND TINK TO PART...
OH, TINK...
I'M SORRY... IT'S FOR YOUR OWN GOOD... SIGH!
AFTER FINDING HER LONG LOST SISTER, IS TINK GOING TO SAY GOODBYE FOREVER?
OKAY, HERE'S THE PLAN. MEET ME HERE TOMORROW... THERE'S SOMETHING I NEED YOU TO BRING...
OH, THANK GOODNESS!
TINKER BELL THINKS SHE HAS IT ALL FIGURED OUT, WHAT COULD POSSIBLY GO WRONG? HER FRIENDS ARE EVEN READY TO HELP...
HER NAME IS PERIWINKLE, AND SHE'S JUST AMAZING! I'M MAKING THIS MACHINE SO SHE CAN COME HERE, AND THEN WE'LL ASK QUEEN CLARION TO CHANGE LORD MILORI'S RULE!
UHM, HAVE YOU THOUGHT THIS THROUGH?
VIDIA!
JUST TELL US WHAT TO DO!
IT'S LIKE YOU'VE FOUND THE PERFECT LOST THING!
AND I'M NEVER GOING TO LOSE HER!

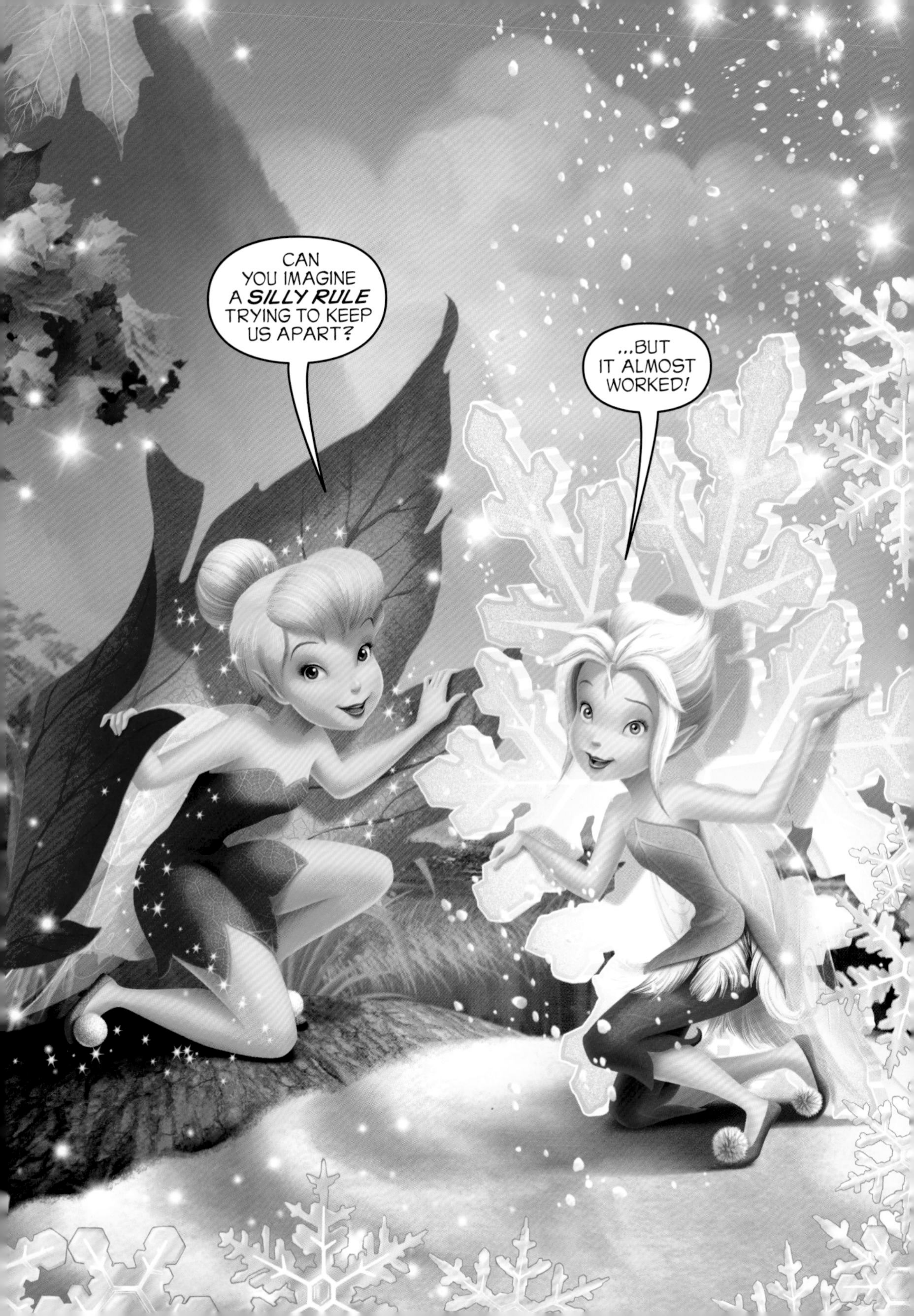
CAN YOU IMAGINE A SILLY RULE TRYING TO KEEP US APART?
...BUT IT ALMOST WORKED!

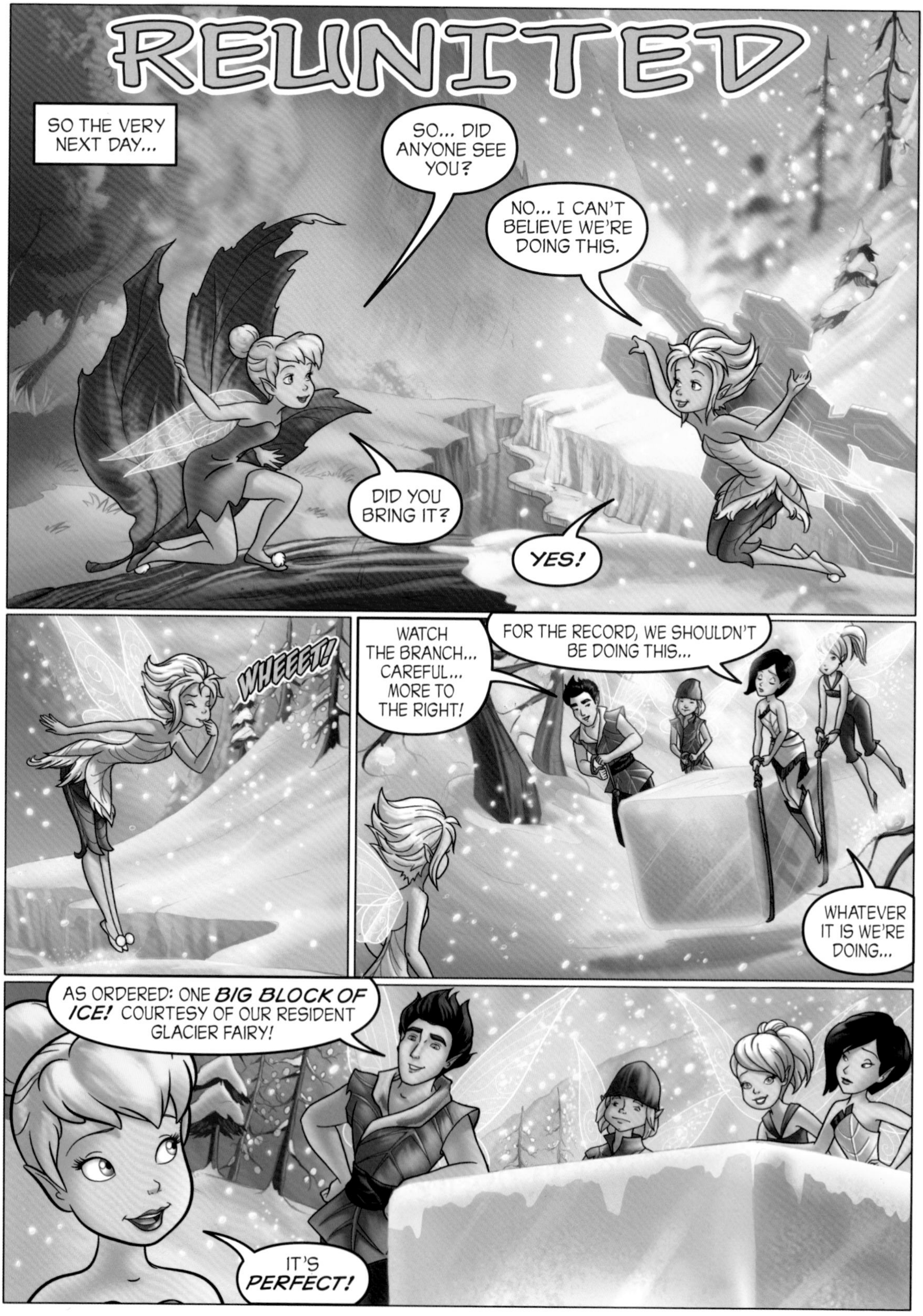
REUNITED
SO THE VERY NEXT DAY...
SO... DID ANYONE SEE YOU?
NO... I CAN'T BELIEVE WE'RE DOING THIS.
DID YOU BRING IT?
YES!
WHEEET!
WATCH THE BRANCH... CAREFUL... MORE TO THE RIGHT!
FOR THE RECORD, WE SHOULDN'T BE DOING THIS...
WHATEVER IT IS WE'RE DOING...
AS ORDERED: ONE BIG BLOCK OF ICE! COURTESY OF OUR RESIDENT GLACIER FAIRY!
IT'S PERFECT!

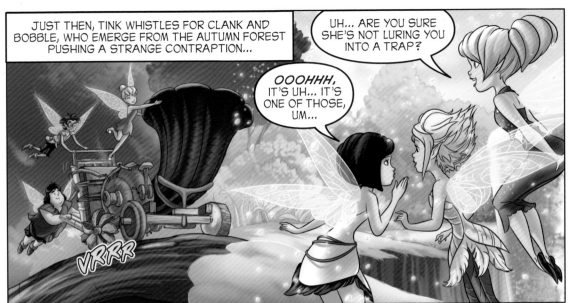

JUST THEN, TINK WHISTLES FOR CLANK AND BOBBLE, WHO EMERGE FROM THE AUTUMN FOREST PUSHING A STRANGE CONTRAPTION...

UH... ARE YOU SURE SHE'S NOT LURING YOU INTO A TRAP?

OOOHHH, IT'S UH... IT'S ONE OF THOSE, UM...

VRRRR

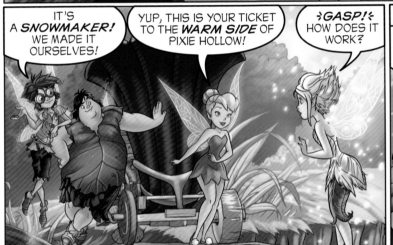

IT'S A *SNOWMAKER!* WE MADE IT OURSELVES!

YUP, THIS IS YOUR TICKET TO THE *WARM SIDE* OF PIXIE HOLLOW!

⚡*GASP!*⚡ HOW DOES IT WORK?

CLANK GRIPS THE BLOCK OF ICE...

YOU MIGHT WANT TO STEP ASIDE FOR THIS PART.

PLINNG

⚡*GASP!*⚡

TINK

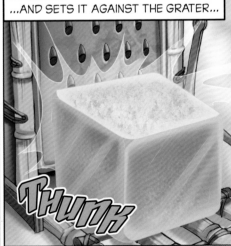

...AND SETS IT AGAINST THE GRATER...

THUNK

NOW BOBBLE CAN START THE SNOWMAKER.

WHRRR

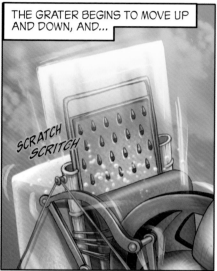

THE GRATER BEGINS TO MOVE UP AND DOWN, AND...

SCRATCH SCRITCH

SNOW SHOOTS INTO THE AIR AND THEN GENTLY DRIFTS BACK DOWN, CREATING A MINI WINTER BEHIND THE SNOWMAKER...

OOO! IT'S COLD! SO...

⁖GASP!⁖ SNOW! YOU DID IT! YOU ACTUALLY DID IT!

THE MACHINE SEEMS TO BE WORKING ALL RIGHT AND EVEN THE WINTER FAIRES APPROVE OF IT...

I DON'T KNOW...

GO, GO ON!

LIVE IT, MAN!

SO TINK'S SISTER MUSTERS THE COURAGE... AND CROSSES THE BORDER.

OHH!

- 36 -

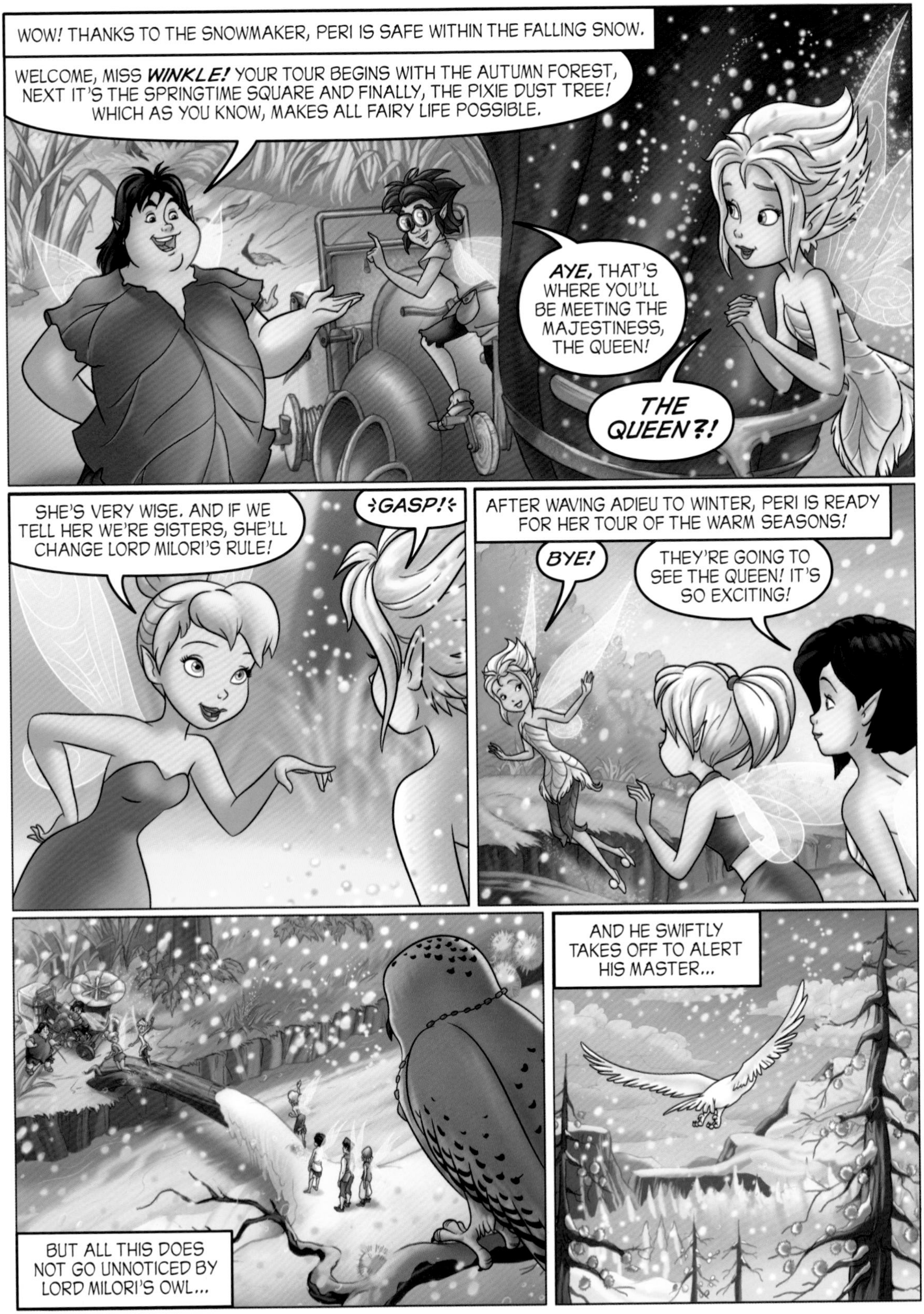
WOW! THANKS TO THE SNOWMAKER, PERI IS SAFE WITHIN THE FALLING SNOW.
WELCOME, MISS *WINKLE!* YOUR TOUR BEGINS WITH THE AUTUMN FOREST, NEXT IT'S THE SPRINGTIME SQUARE AND FINALLY, THE PIXIE DUST TREE! WHICH AS YOU KNOW, MAKES ALL FAIRY LIFE POSSIBLE.
AYE, THAT'S WHERE YOU'LL BE MEETING THE MAJESTINESS, THE QUEEN!
THE QUEEN?!
SHE'S VERY WISE. AND IF WE TELL HER WE'RE SISTERS, SHE'LL CHANGE LORD MILORI'S RULE!
GASP!
AFTER WAVING ADIEU TO WINTER, PERI IS READY FOR HER TOUR OF THE WARM SEASONS!
BYE!
THEY'RE GOING TO SEE THE QUEEN! IT'S SO EXCITING!
BUT ALL THIS DOES NOT GO UNNOTICED BY LORD MILORI'S OWL...
AND HE SWIFTLY TAKES OFF TO ALERT HIS MASTER...

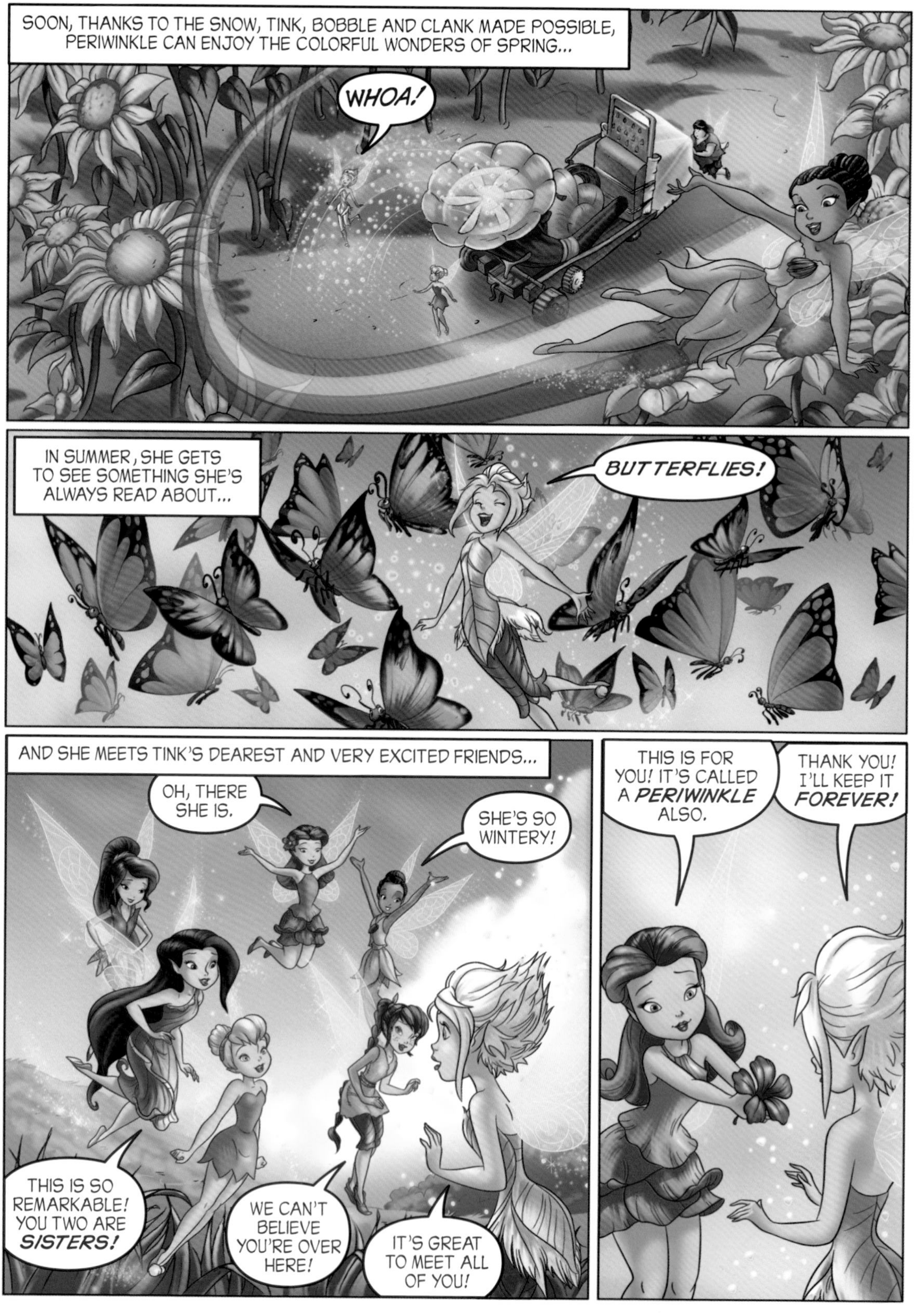
SOON, THANKS TO THE SNOW, TINK, BOBBLE AND CLANK MADE POSSIBLE, PERIWINKLE CAN ENJOY THE COLORFUL WONDERS OF SPRING...
WHOA!
IN SUMMER, SHE GETS TO SEE SOMETHING SHE'S ALWAYS READ ABOUT...
BUTTERFLIES!
AND SHE MEETS TINK'S DEAREST AND VERY EXCITED FRIENDS...
OH, THERE SHE IS.
SHE'S SO WINTERY!
THIS IS SO REMARKABLE! YOU TWO ARE SISTERS!
WE CAN'T BELIEVE YOU'RE OVER HERE!
IT'S GREAT TO MEET ALL OF YOU!
THIS IS FOR YOU! IT'S CALLED A PERIWINKLE ALSO.
THANK YOU! I'LL KEEP IT FOREVER!

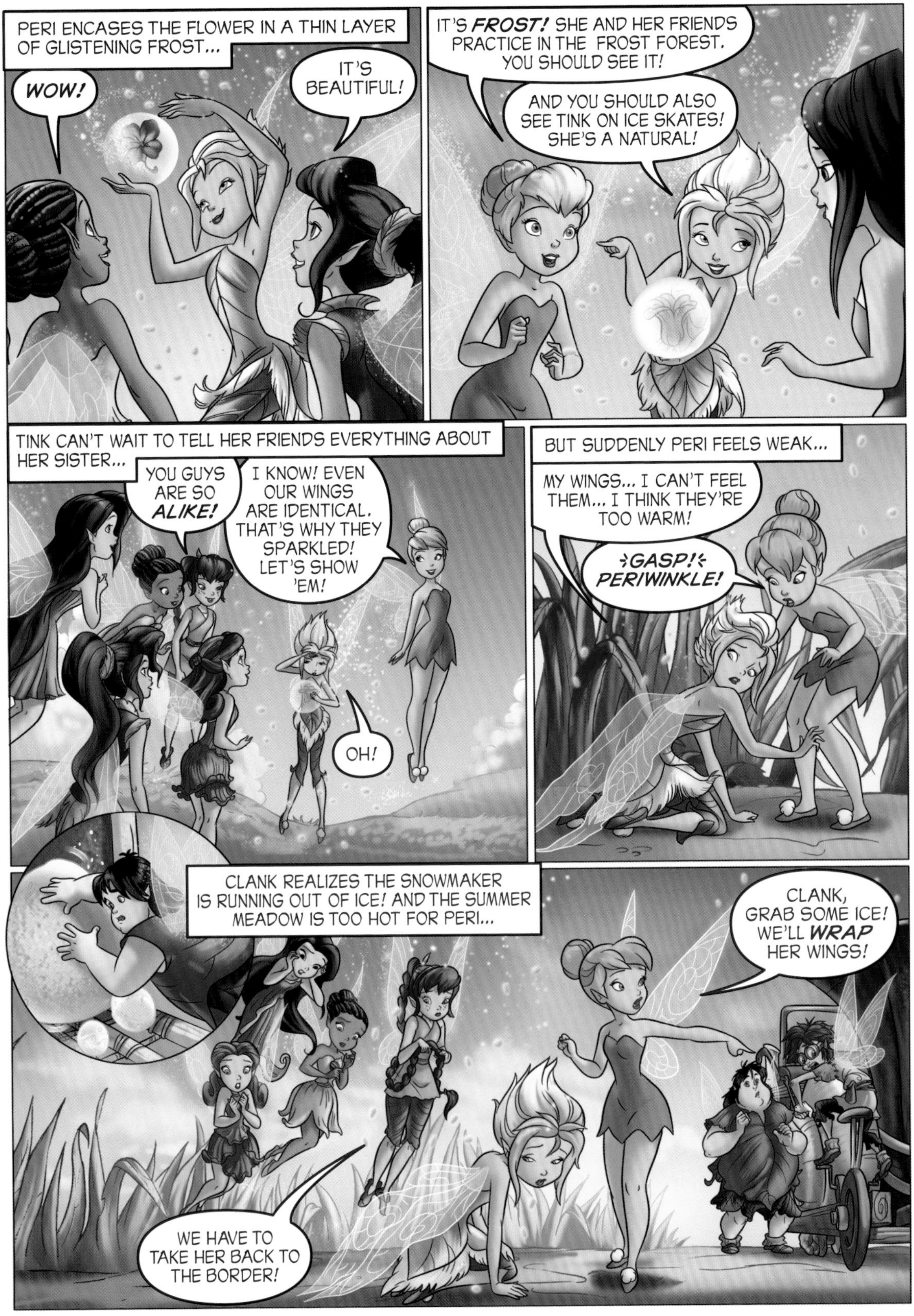
PERI ENCASES THE FLOWER IN A THIN LAYER OF GLISTENING FROST...
WOW!
IT'S BEAUTIFUL!
IT'S FROST! SHE AND HER FRIENDS PRACTICE IN THE FROST FOREST. YOU SHOULD SEE IT!
AND YOU SHOULD ALSO SEE TINK ON ICE SKATES! SHE'S A NATURAL!
TINK CAN'T WAIT TO TELL HER FRIENDS EVERYTHING ABOUT HER SISTER...
YOU GUYS ARE SO ALIKE!
I KNOW! EVEN OUR WINGS ARE IDENTICAL. THAT'S WHY THEY SPARKLED! LET'S SHOW 'EM!
OH!
BUT SUDDENLY PERI FEELS WEAK...
MY WINGS... I CAN'T FEEL THEM... I THINK THEY'RE TOO WARM!
GASP! PERIWINKLE!
CLANK REALIZES THE SNOWMAKER IS RUNNING OUT OF ICE! AND THE SUMMER MEADOW IS TOO HOT FOR PERI...
CLANK, GRAB SOME ICE! WE'LL WRAP HER WINGS!
WE HAVE TO TAKE HER BACK TO THE BORDER!

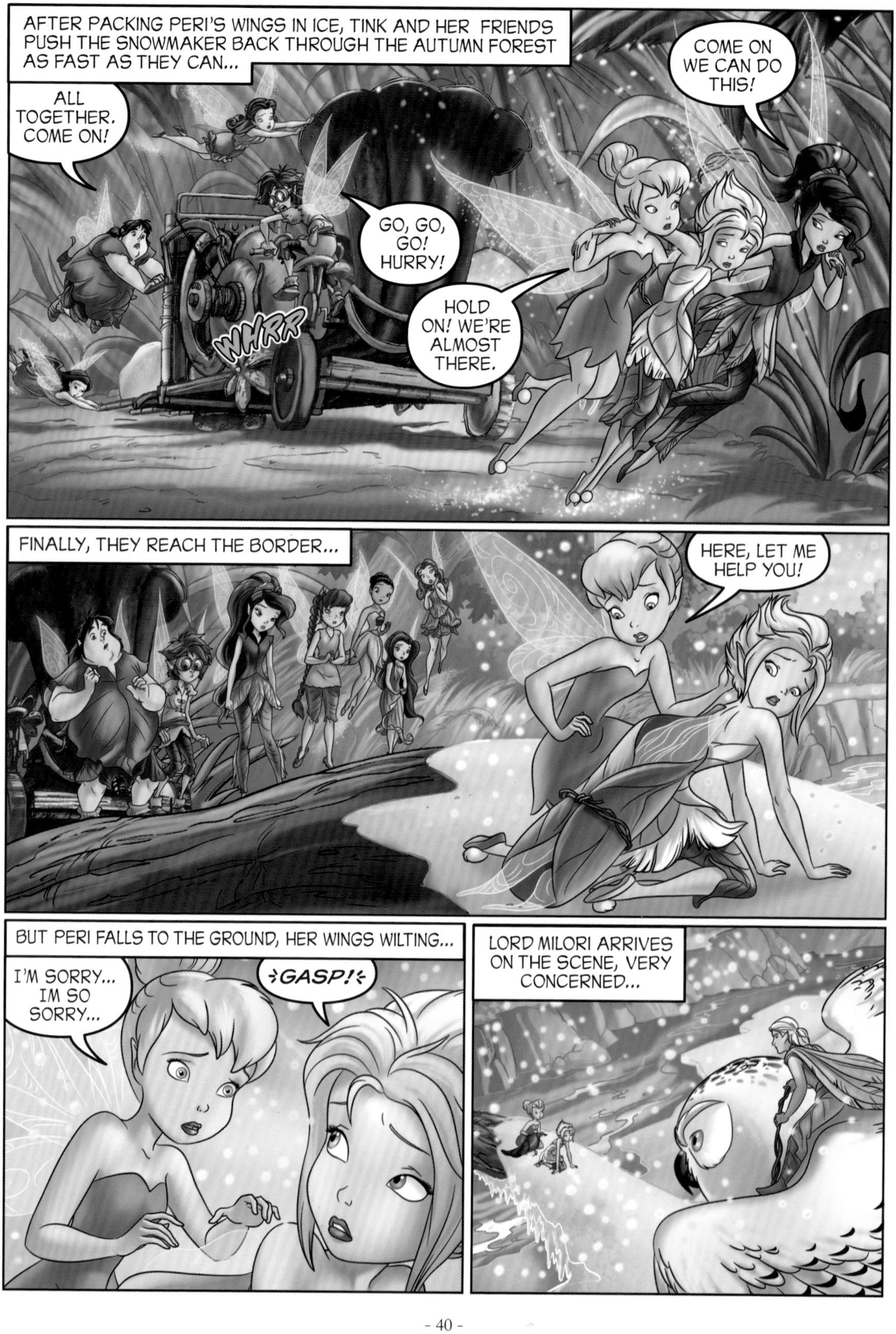
AFTER PACKING PERI'S WINGS IN ICE, TINK AND HER FRIENDS PUSH THE SNOWMAKER BACK THROUGH THE AUTUMN FOREST AS FAST AS THEY CAN...
ALL TOGETHER. COME ON!
GO, GO, GO! HURRY!
WHRR
HOLD ON! WE'RE ALMOST THERE.
COME ON WE CAN DO THIS!
FINALLY, THEY REACH THE BORDER...
HERE, LET ME HELP YOU!
BUT PERI FALLS TO THE GROUND, HER WINGS WILTING...
I'M SORRY... IM SO SORRY...
GASP!
LORD MILORI ARRIVES ON THE SCENE, VERY CONCERNED...

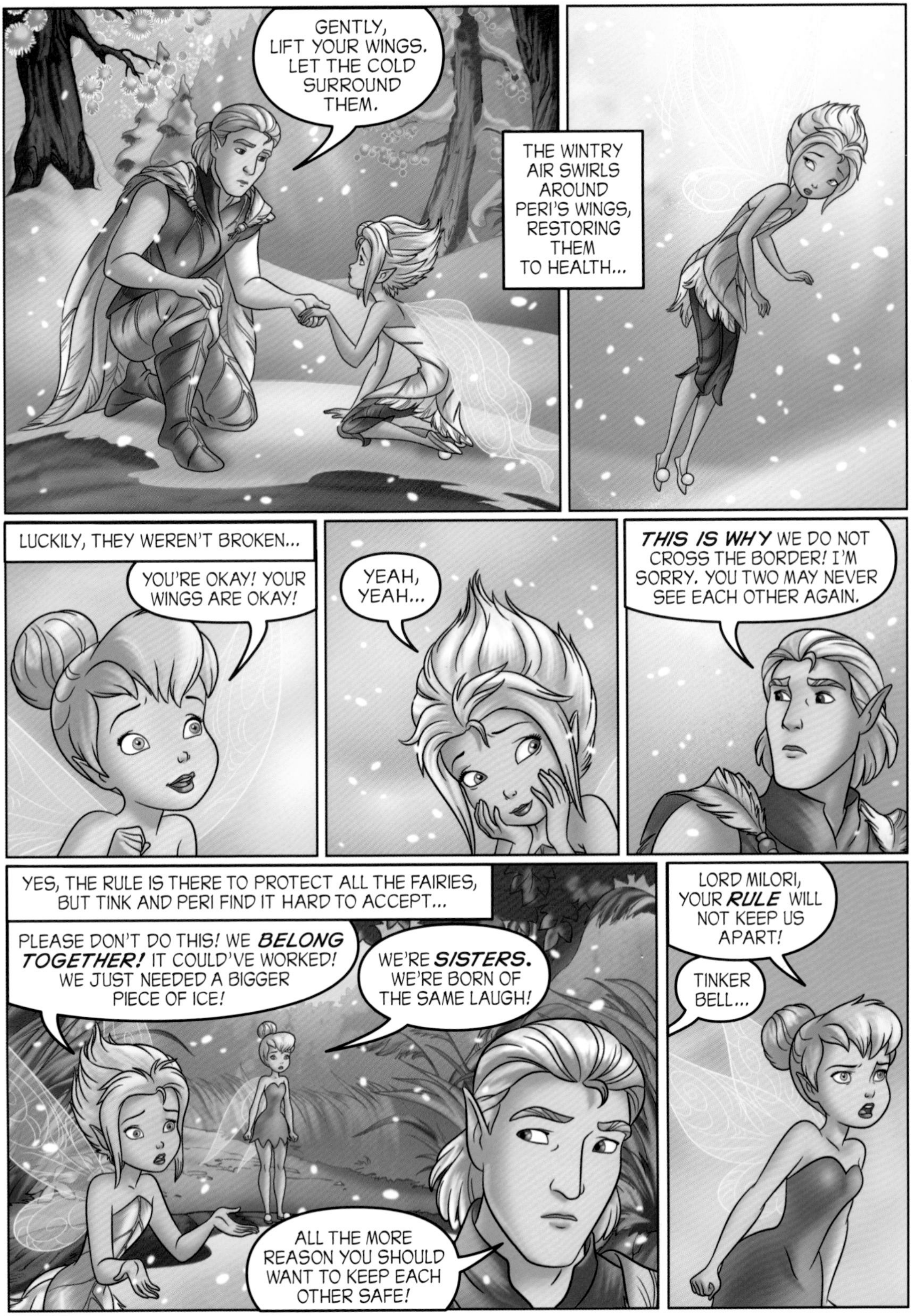
GENTLY, LIFT YOUR WINGS. LET THE COLD SURROUND THEM.
THE WINTRY AIR SWIRLS AROUND PERI'S WINGS, RESTORING THEM TO HEALTH...
LUCKILY, THEY WEREN'T BROKEN...
YOU'RE OKAY! YOUR WINGS ARE OKAY!
YEAH, YEAH...
THIS IS WHY WE DO NOT CROSS THE BORDER! I'M SORRY. YOU TWO MAY NEVER SEE EACH OTHER AGAIN.
YES, THE RULE IS THERE TO PROTECT ALL THE FAIRIES, BUT TINK AND PERI FIND IT HARD TO ACCEPT...
PLEASE DON'T DO THIS! WE BELONG TOGETHER! IT COULD'VE WORKED! WE JUST NEEDED A BIGGER PIECE OF ICE!
WE'RE SISTERS. WE'RE BORN OF THE SAME LAUGH!
ALL THE MORE REASON YOU SHOULD WANT TO KEEP EACH OTHER SAFE!
LORD MILORI, YOUR RULE WILL NOT KEEP US APART!
TINKER BELL...

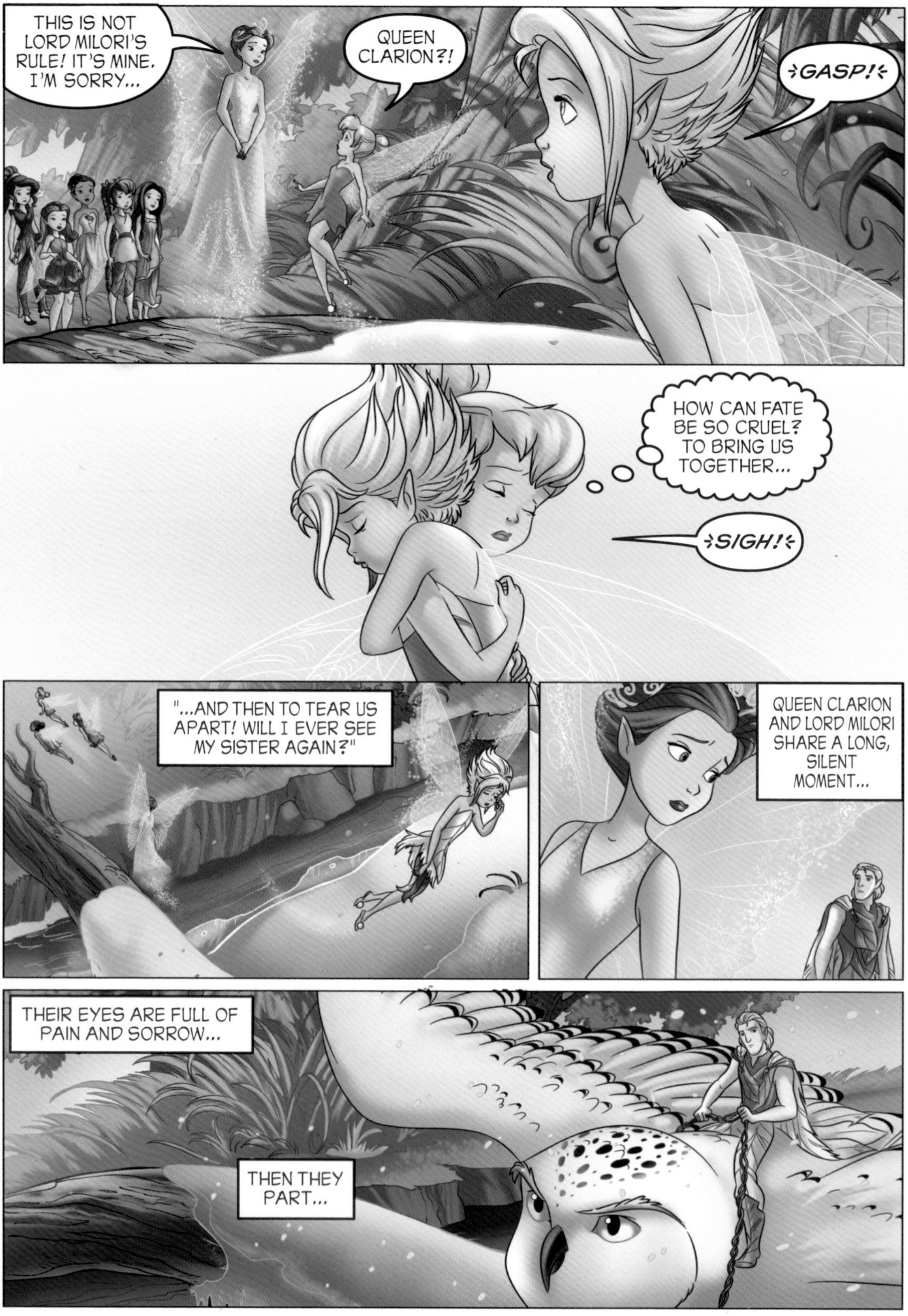
THIS IS NOT LORD MILORI'S RULE! IT'S MINE. I'M SORRY...
QUEEN CLARION?!
GASP!
HOW CAN FATE BE SO CRUEL? TO BRING US TOGETHER...
SIGH!
"...AND THEN TO TEAR US APART! WILL I EVER SEE MY SISTER AGAIN?"
QUEEN CLARION AND LORD MILORI SHARE A LONG, SILENT MOMENT...
THEIR EYES ARE FULL OF PAIN AND SORROW...
THEN THEY PART...

BEFORE LEAVING, LORD MILORI CASTS ASIDE THE SNOWMAKER...

BUT UNSEEN BY THE LORD OF WINTER, THE SNOWMAKER GETS STUCK ON A LEDGE OVER A SMALL WATERFALL...

SPLASH

...AND ICE FLOES CONTINUE TO FEED THE MACHINE AS A BLIZZARD OF SNOW PUMPS INTO THE SKY...

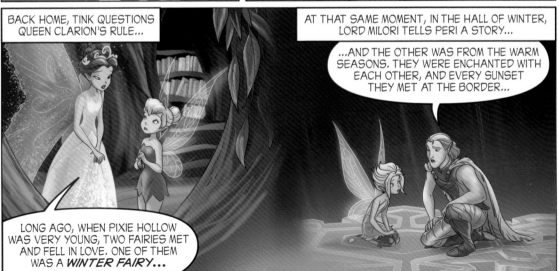

BACK HOME, TINK QUESTIONS QUEEN CLARION'S RULE...

LONG AGO, WHEN PIXIE HOLLOW WAS VERY YOUNG, TWO FAIRIES MET AND FELL IN LOVE. ONE OF THEM WAS A *WINTER FAIRY*...

AT THAT SAME MOMENT, IN THE HALL OF WINTER, LORD MILORI TELLS PERI A STORY...

...AND THE OTHER WAS FROM THE WARM SEASONS. THEY WERE ENCHANTED WITH EACH OTHER, AND EVERY SUNSET THEY MET AT THE BORDER...

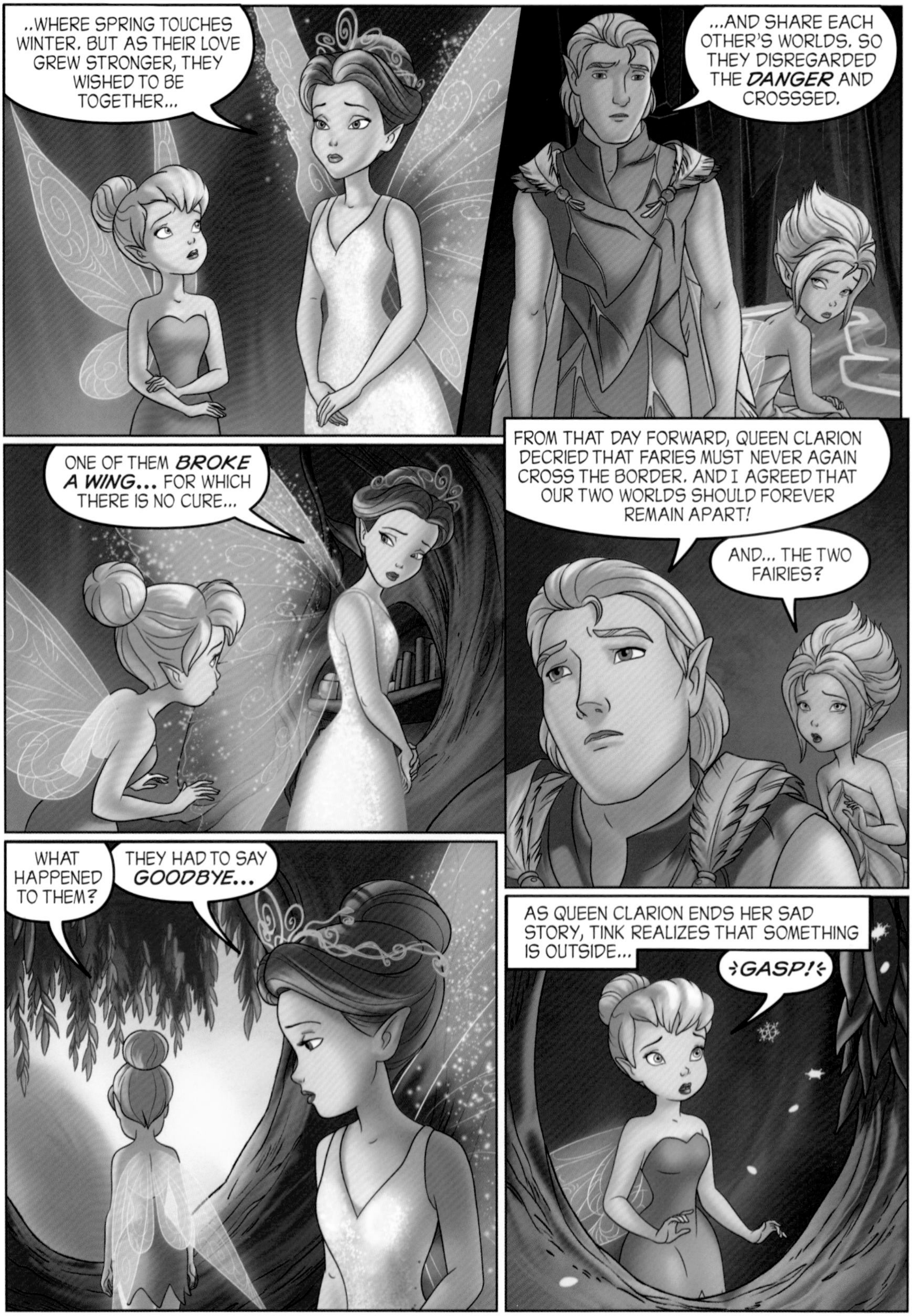
..WHERE SPRING TOUCHES WINTER. BUT AS THEIR LOVE GREW STRONGER, THEY WISHED TO BE TOGETHER...
...AND SHARE EACH OTHER'S WORLDS. SO THEY DISREGARDED THE DANGER AND CROSSSED.
ONE OF THEM BROKE A WING... FOR WHICH THERE IS NO CURE...
FROM THAT DAY FORWARD, QUEEN CLARION DECRIED THAT FARIES MUST NEVER AGAIN CROSS THE BORDER. AND I AGREED THAT OUR TWO WORLDS SHOULD FOREVER REMAIN APART!
AND... THE TWO FAIRIES?
WHAT HAPPENED TO THEM?
THEY HAD TO SAY GOODBYE...
AS QUEEN CLARION ENDS HER SAD STORY, TINK REALIZES THAT SOMETHING IS OUTSIDE...
GASP!

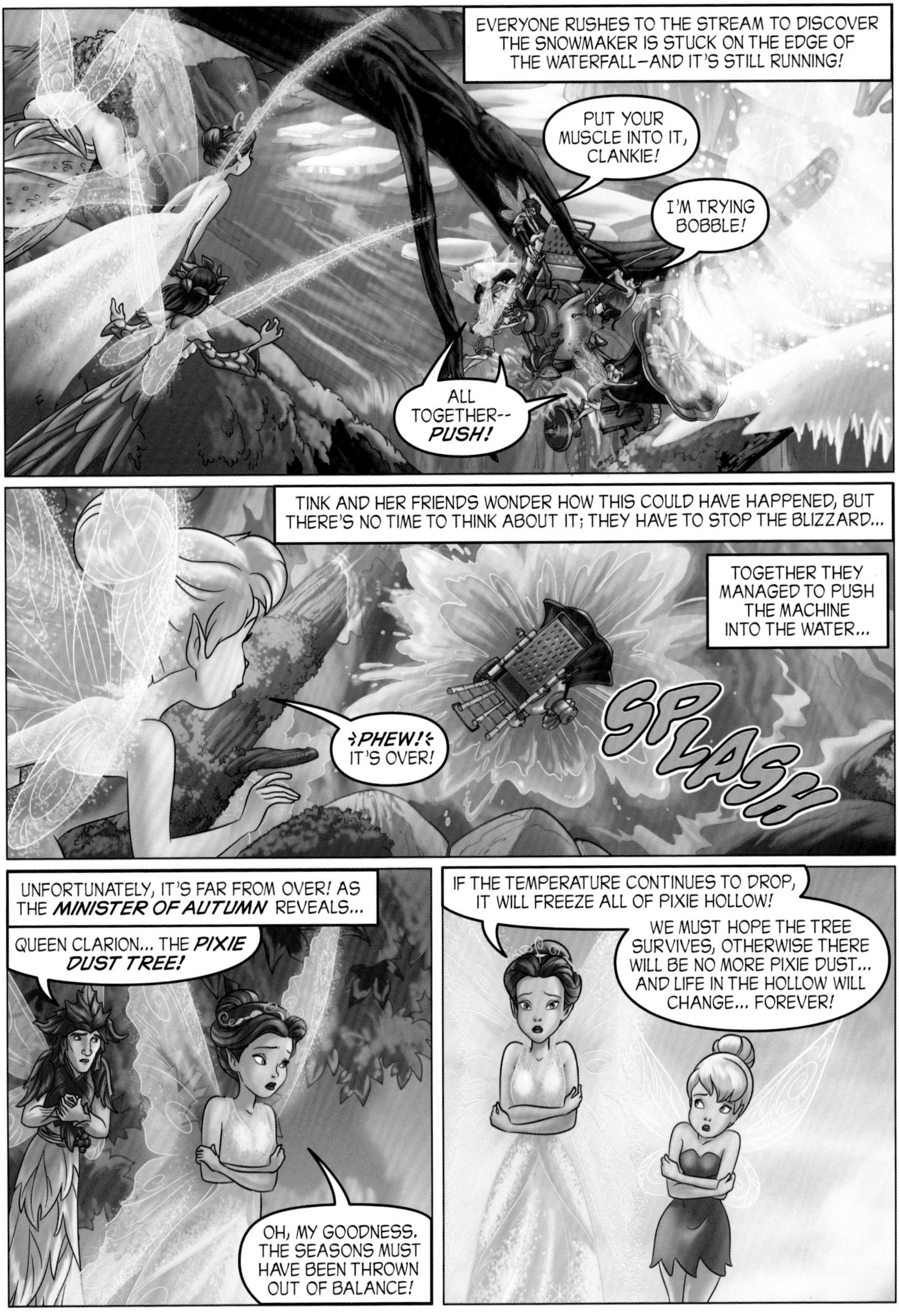
EVERYONE RUSHES TO THE STREAM TO DISCOVER THE SNOWMAKER IS STUCK ON THE EDGE OF THE WATERFALL—AND IT'S STILL RUNNING!
PUT YOUR MUSCLE INTO IT, CLANKIE!
I'M TRYING BOBBLE!
ALL TOGETHER-- PUSH!
TINK AND HER FRIENDS WONDER HOW THIS COULD HAVE HAPPENED, BUT THERE'S NO TIME TO THINK ABOUT IT; THEY HAVE TO STOP THE BLIZZARD...
TOGETHER THEY MANAGED TO PUSH THE MACHINE INTO THE WATER...
PHEW! IT'S OVER!
SPLASH
UNFORTUNATELY, IT'S FAR FROM OVER! AS THE MINISTER OF AUTUMN REVEALS...
QUEEN CLARION... THE PIXIE DUST TREE!
OH, MY GOODNESS. THE SEASONS MUST HAVE BEEN THROWN OUT OF BALANCE!
IF THE TEMPERATURE CONTINUES TO DROP, IT WILL FREEZE ALL OF PIXIE HOLLOW!
WE MUST HOPE THE TREE SURVIVES, OTHERWISE THERE WILL BE NO MORE PIXIE DUST... AND LIFE IN THE HOLLOW WILL CHANGE... FOREVER!

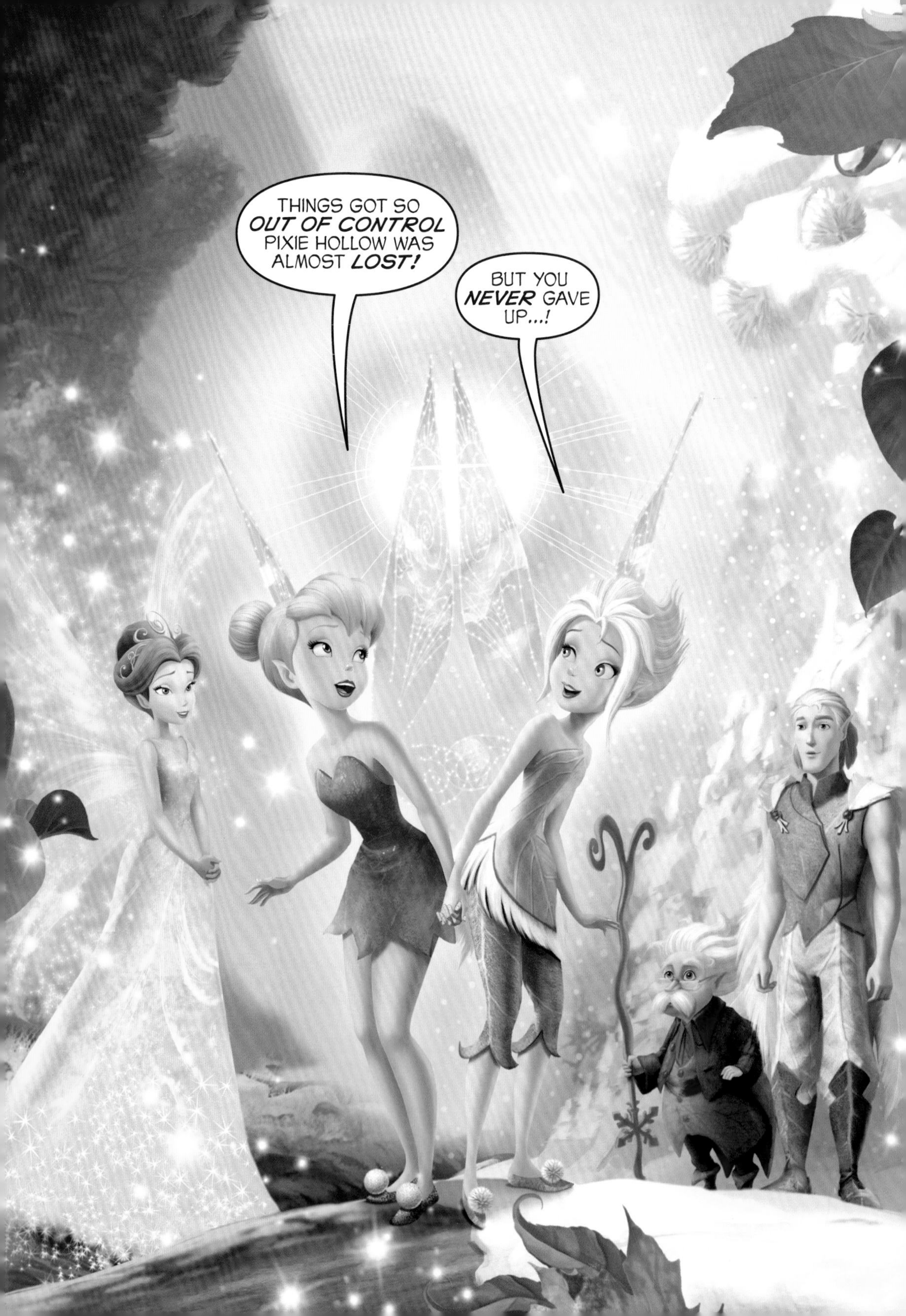
THINGS GOT SO OUT OF CONTROL PIXIE HOLLOW WAS ALMOST LOST!
BUT YOU NEVER GAVE UP...!

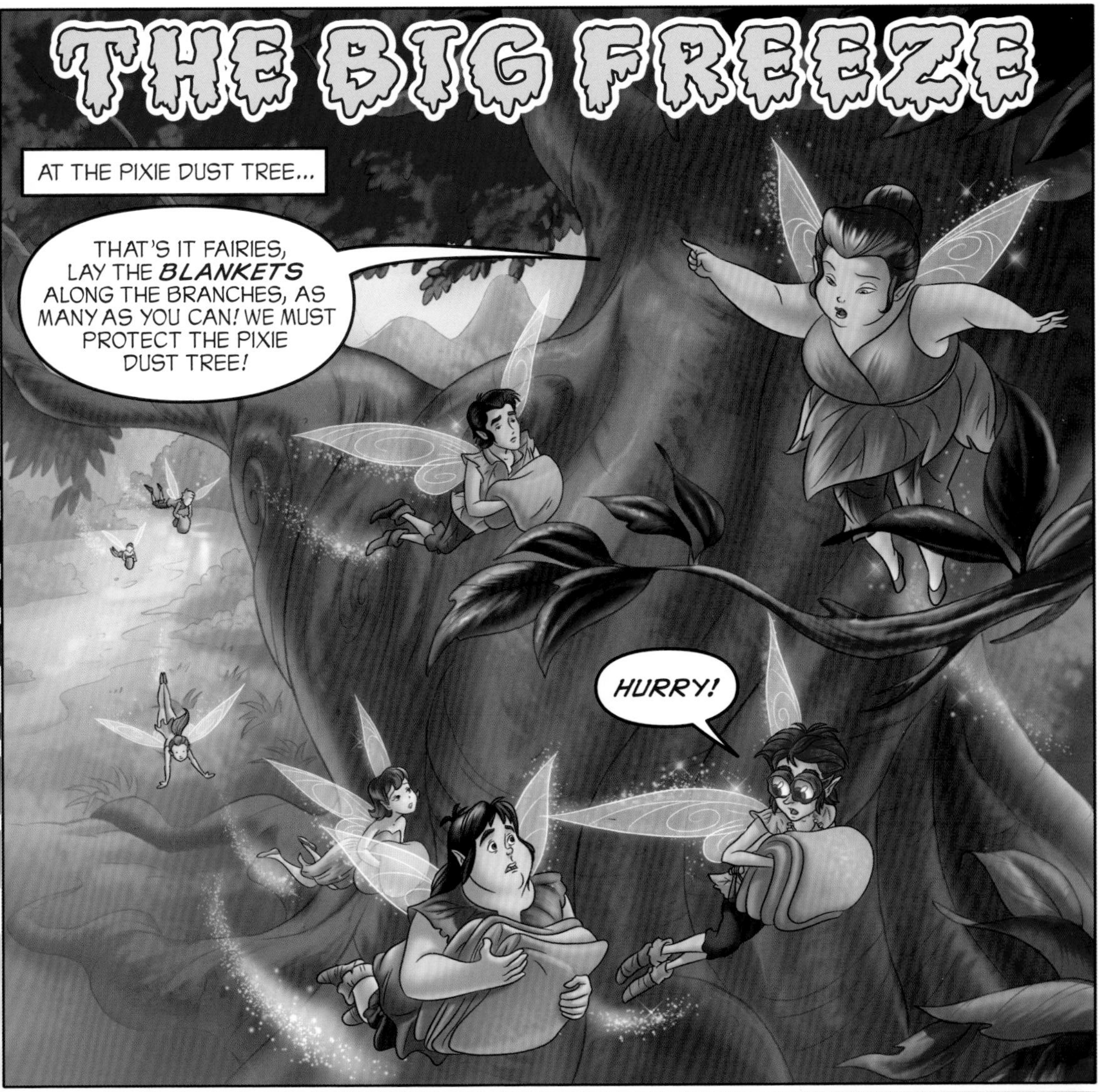
THE BIG FREEZE
AT THE PIXIE DUST TREE...
THAT'S IT FAIRIES, LAY THE BLANKETS ALONG THE BRANCHES, AS MANY AS YOU CAN! WE MUST PROTECT THE PIXIE DUST TREE!
HURRY!

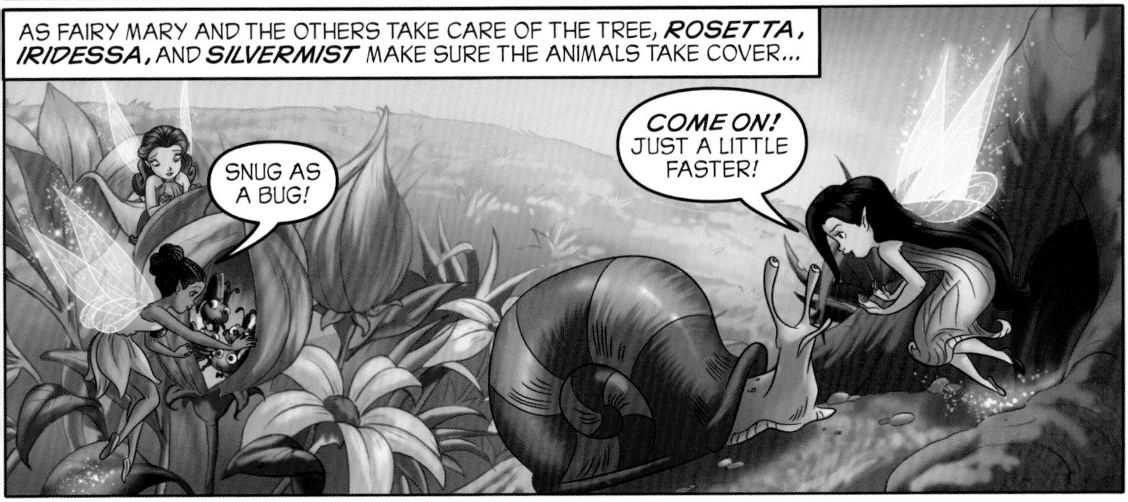
AS FAIRY MARY AND THE OTHERS TAKE CARE OF THE TREE, ROSETTA, IRIDESSA, AND SILVERMIST MAKE SURE THE ANIMALS TAKE COVER...
SNUG AS A BUG!
COME ON! JUST A LITTLE FASTER!

TINK IS HELPING SOME LITTLE FRIENDS TOO...

YOU GUYS JUST STAY HERE AND KEEP WARM.

EVERYTHING'S GOING TO BE--

JUST THEN, SOMETHING EXTRAORDINARY CATCHES HER ATTENTION...

...FINE... HUH?!

CRACK

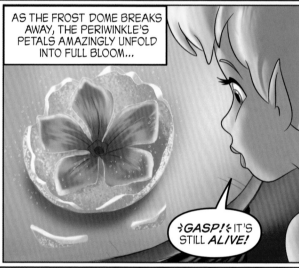

AS THE FROST DOME BREAKS AWAY, THE PERIWINKLE'S PETALS AMAZINGLY UNFOLD INTO FULL BLOOM...

≩GASP!≩ IT'S STILL *ALIVE!*

AND TINK GETS A FLITTERIFIC IDEA THAT COULD JUST SAVE HER WORLD!

PERI!

IN THE MEANTIME, THE WINTER PIXIE DUST SUPPLY HAS NEARLY DRIED UP...

THERE MUST BE SOMETHING **WRONG** WITH THE PIXIE DUST TREE!

OH, DEAR!

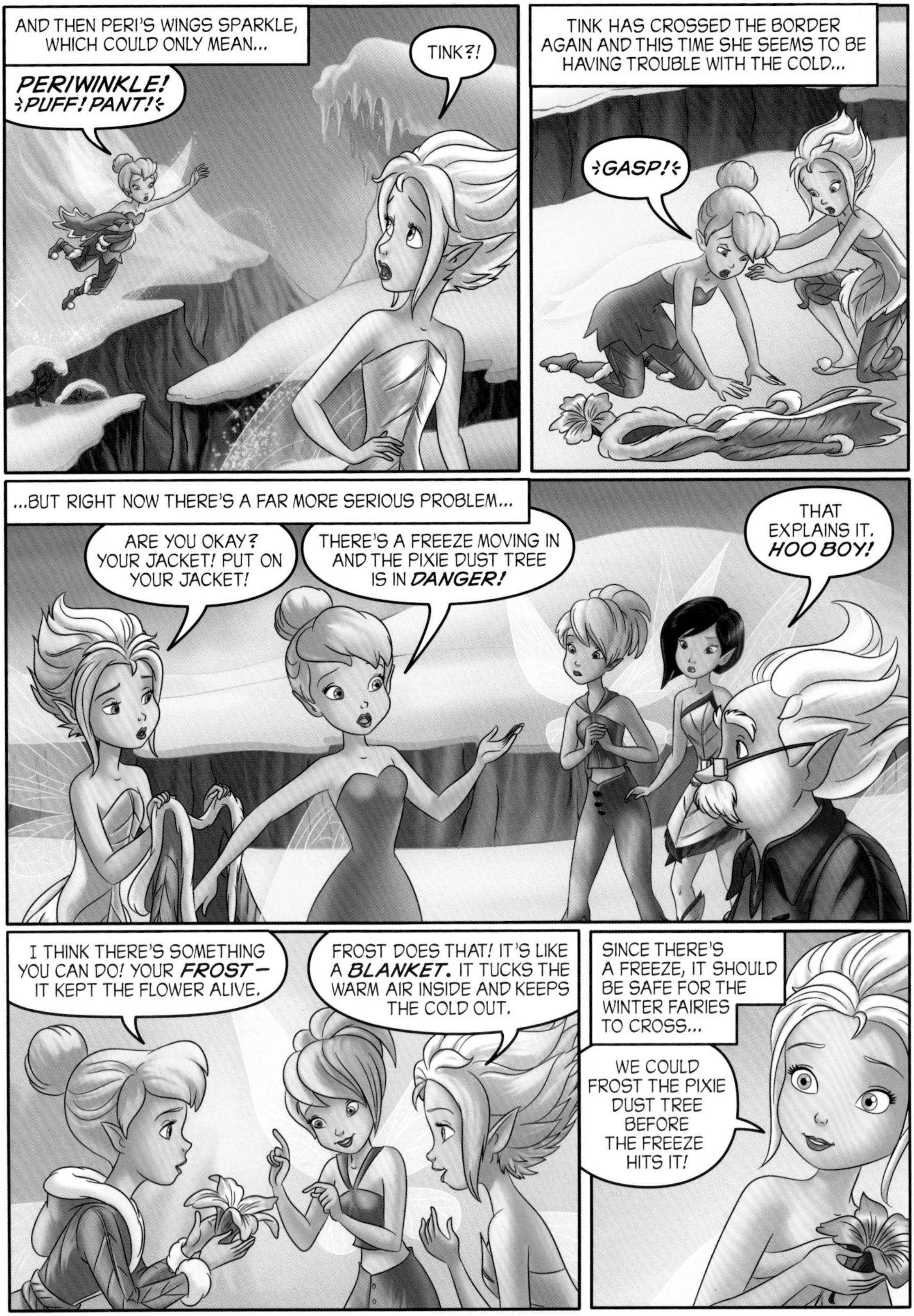

AND THEN PERI'S WINGS SPARKLE, WHICH COULD ONLY MEAN...
PERIWINKLE! ⁘PUFF! PANT!⁘
TINK?!
TINK HAS CROSSED THE BORDER AGAIN AND THIS TIME SHE SEEMS TO BE HAVING TROUBLE WITH THE COLD...
⁘GASP!⁘
...BUT RIGHT NOW THERE'S A FAR MORE SERIOUS PROBLEM...
ARE YOU OKAY? YOUR JACKET! PUT ON YOUR JACKET!
THERE'S A FREEZE MOVING IN AND THE PIXIE DUST TREE IS IN DANGER!
THAT EXPLAINS IT. HOO BOY!
I THINK THERE'S SOMETHING YOU CAN DO! YOUR FROST— IT KEPT THE FLOWER ALIVE.
FROST DOES THAT! IT'S LIKE A BLANKET. IT TUCKS THE WARM AIR INSIDE AND KEEPS THE COLD OUT.
SINCE THERE'S A FREEZE, IT SHOULD BE SAFE FOR THE WINTER FAIRIES TO CROSS...
WE COULD FROST THE PIXIE DUST TREE BEFORE THE FREEZE HITS IT!

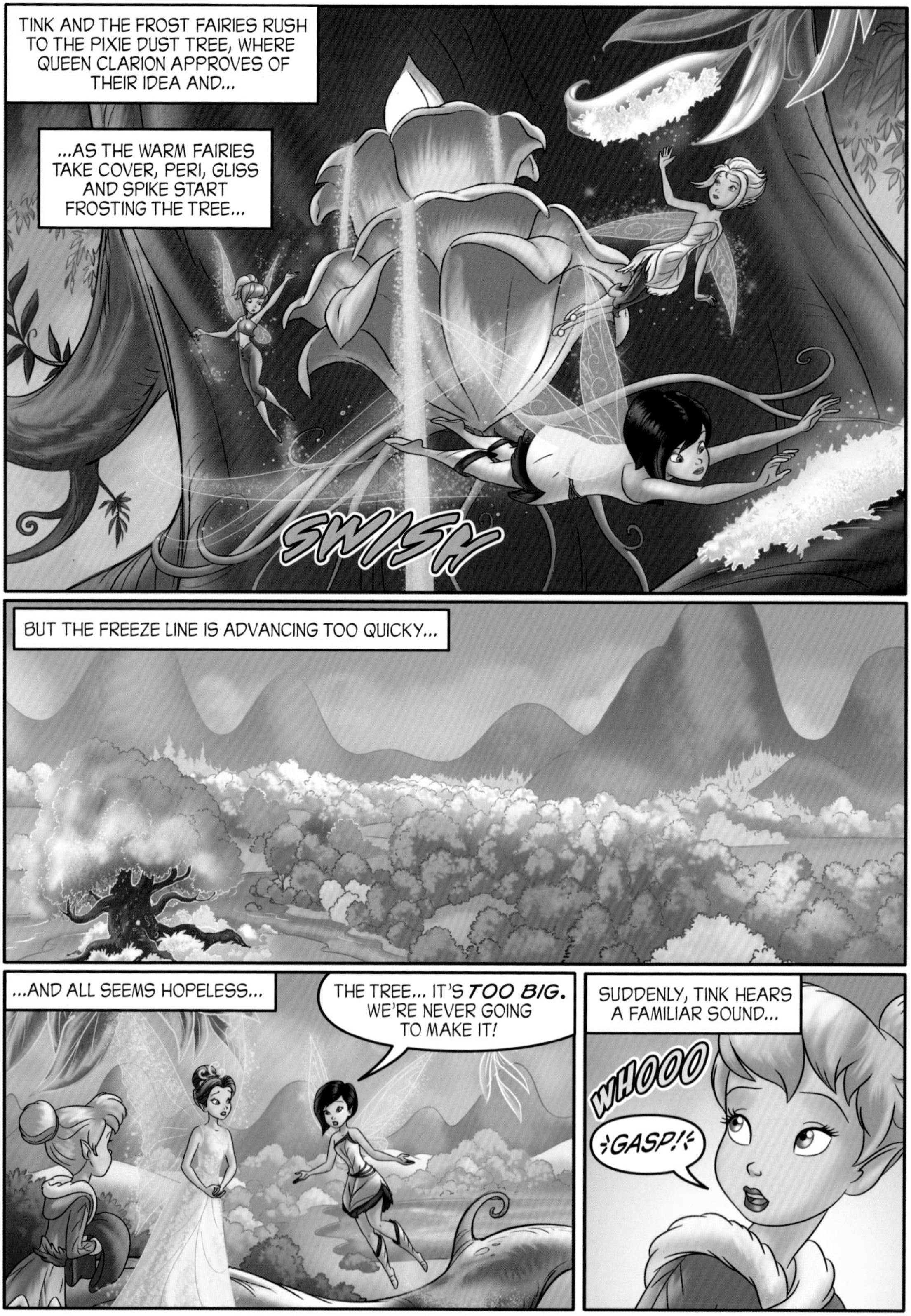

TINK AND THE FROST FAIRIES RUSH TO THE PIXIE DUST TREE, WHERE QUEEN CLARION APPROVES OF THEIR IDEA AND...
...AS THE WARM FAIRIES TAKE COVER, PERI, GLISS AND SPIKE START FROSTING THE TREE...
SWISH
BUT THE FREEZE LINE IS ADVANCING TOO QUICKY...
...AND ALL SEEMS HOPELESS...
THE TREE... IT'S **TOO BIG.** WE'RE NEVER GOING TO MAKE IT!
SUDDENLY, TINK HEARS A FAMILIAR SOUND...
WHOOO
GASP!

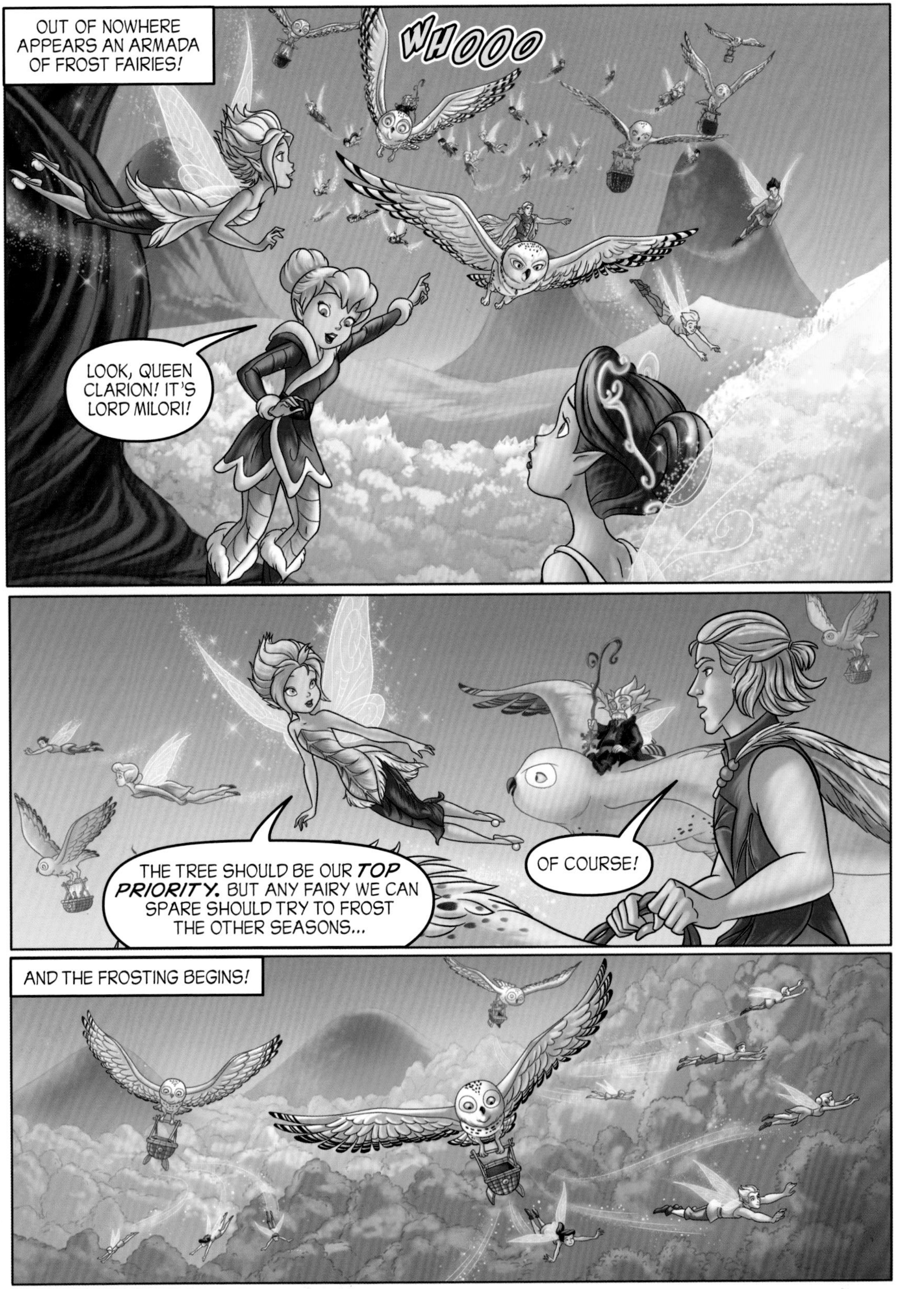
OUT OF NOWHERE APPEARS AN ARMADA OF FROST FAIRIES!
WHOOO
LOOK, QUEEN CLARION! IT'S LORD MILORI!
THE TREE SHOULD BE OUR TOP PRIORITY. BUT ANY FAIRY WE CAN SPARE SHOULD TRY TO FROST THE OTHER SEASONS...
OF COURSE!
AND THE FROSTING BEGINS!

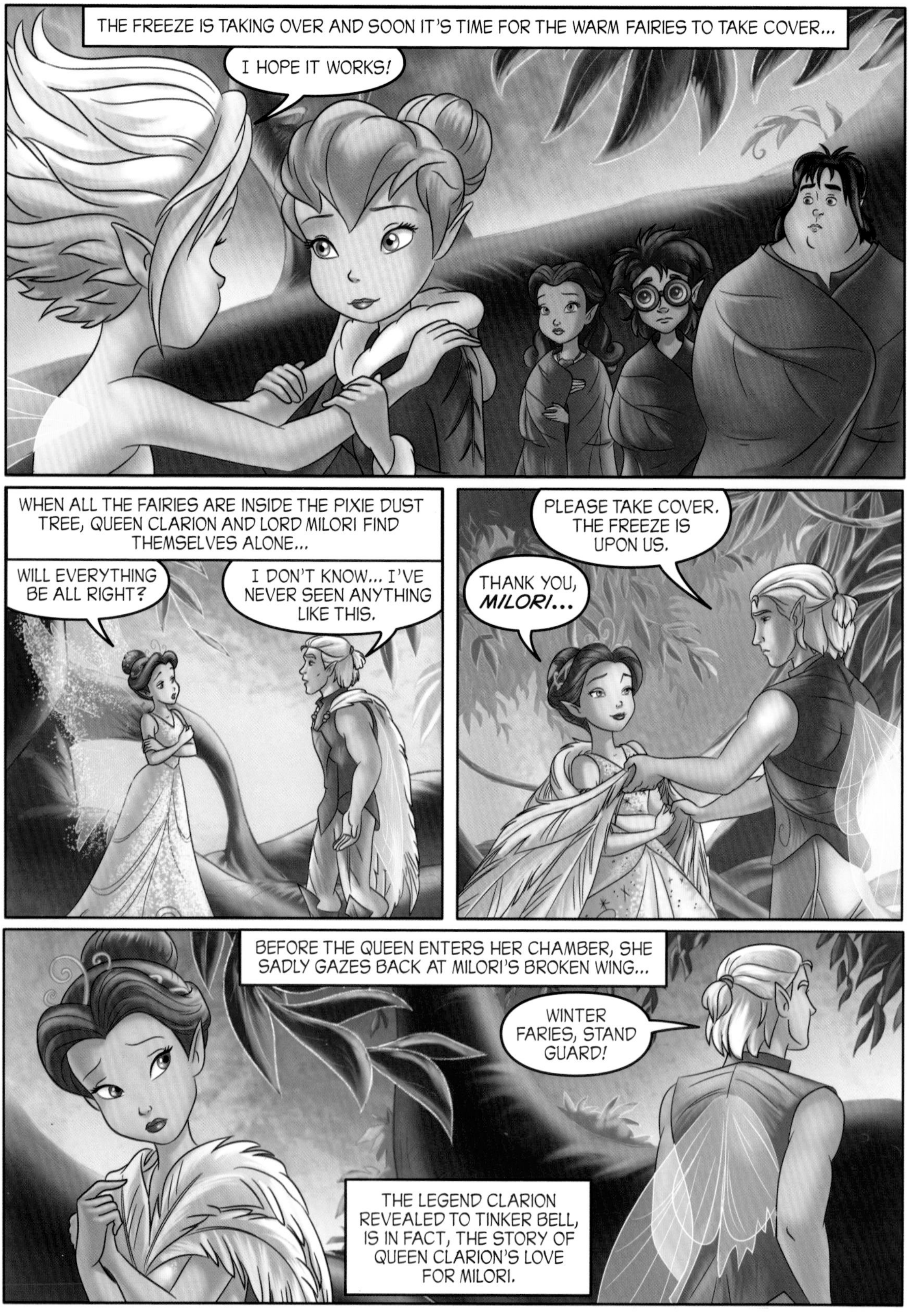
THE FREEZE IS TAKING OVER AND SOON IT'S TIME FOR THE WARM FAIRIES TO TAKE COVER...
I HOPE IT WORKS!
WHEN ALL THE FAIRIES ARE INSIDE THE PIXIE DUST TREE, QUEEN CLARION AND LORD MILORI FIND THEMSELVES ALONE...
WILL EVERYTHING BE ALL RIGHT?
I DON'T KNOW... I'VE NEVER SEEN ANYTHING LIKE THIS.
PLEASE TAKE COVER. THE FREEZE IS UPON US.
THANK YOU, MILORI...
BEFORE THE QUEEN ENTERS HER CHAMBER, SHE SADLY GAZES BACK AT MILORI'S BROKEN WING...
WINTER FARIES, STAND GUARD!
THE LEGEND CLARION REVEALED TO TINKER BELL, IS IN FACT, THE STORY OF QUEEN CLARION'S LOVE FOR MILORI.

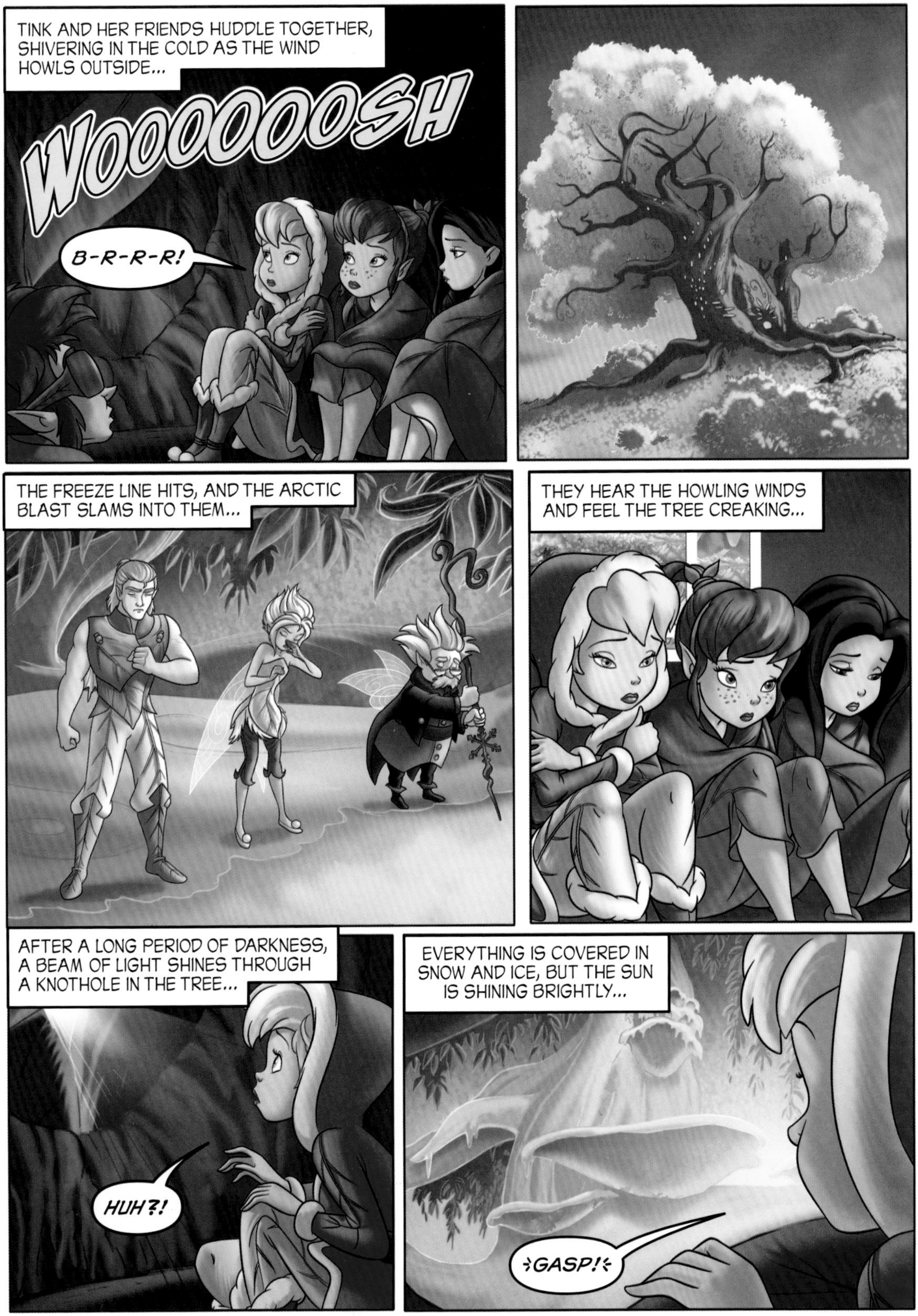

TINK AND HER FRIENDS HUDDLE TOGETHER, SHIVERING IN THE COLD AS THE WIND HOWLS OUTSIDE...
WOOOOOOSH
B-R-R-R!
THE FREEZE LINE HITS, AND THE ARCTIC BLAST SLAMS INTO THEM...
THEY HEAR THE HOWLING WINDS AND FEEL THE TREE CREAKING...
AFTER A LONG PERIOD OF DARKNESS, A BEAM OF LIGHT SHINES THROUGH A KNOTHOLE IN THE TREE...
HUH?!
EVERYTHING IS COVERED IN SNOW AND ICE, BUT THE SUN IS SHINING BRIGHTLY...
GASP!

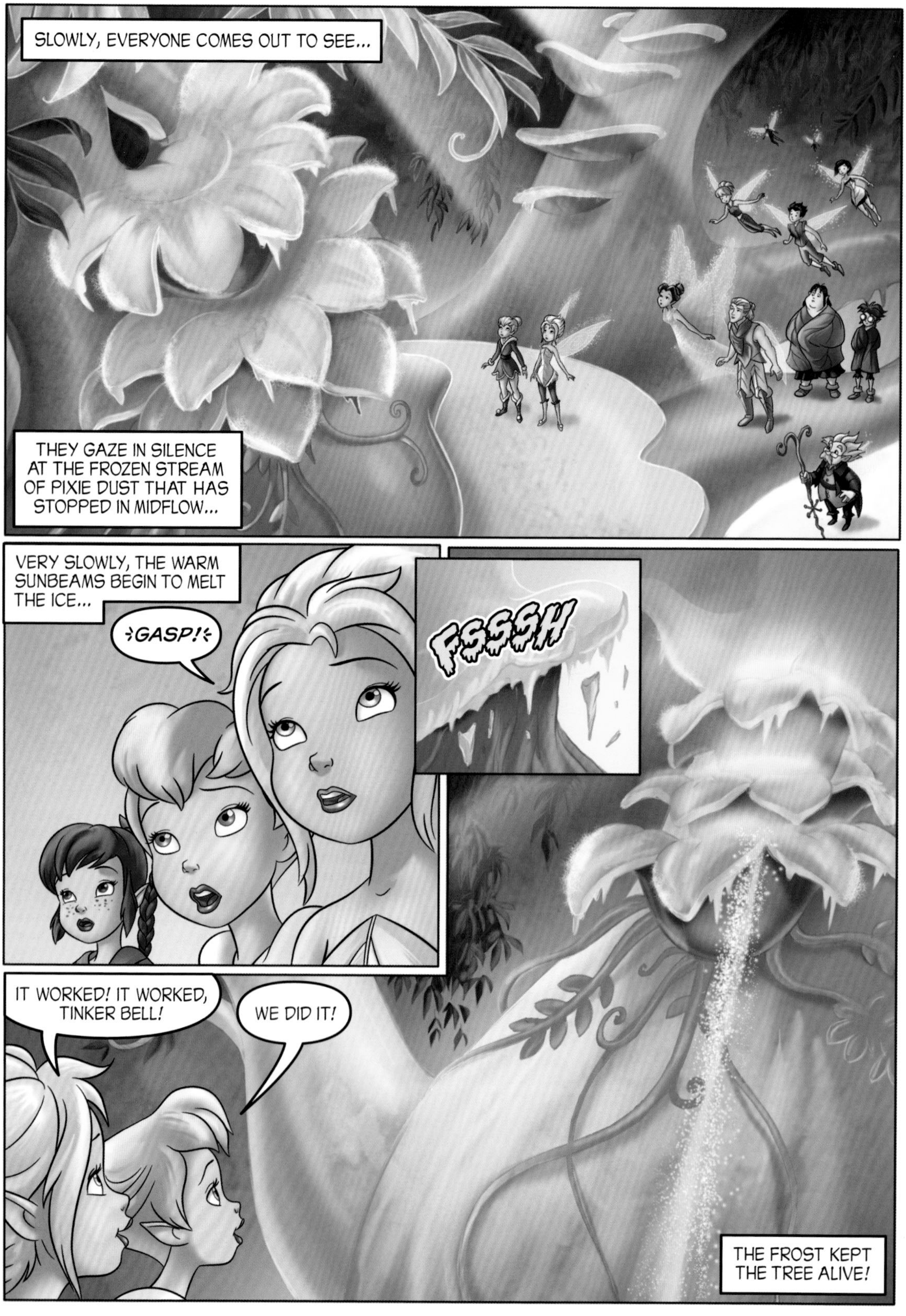
SLOWLY, EVERYONE COMES OUT TO SEE...
THEY GAZE IN SILENCE AT THE FROZEN STREAM OF PIXIE DUST THAT HAS STOPPED IN MIDFLOW...
VERY SLOWLY, THE WARM SUNBEAMS BEGIN TO MELT THE ICE...
GASP!
FSSSH
IT WORKED! IT WORKED, TINKER BELL!
WE DID IT!
THE FROST KEPT THE TREE ALIVE!

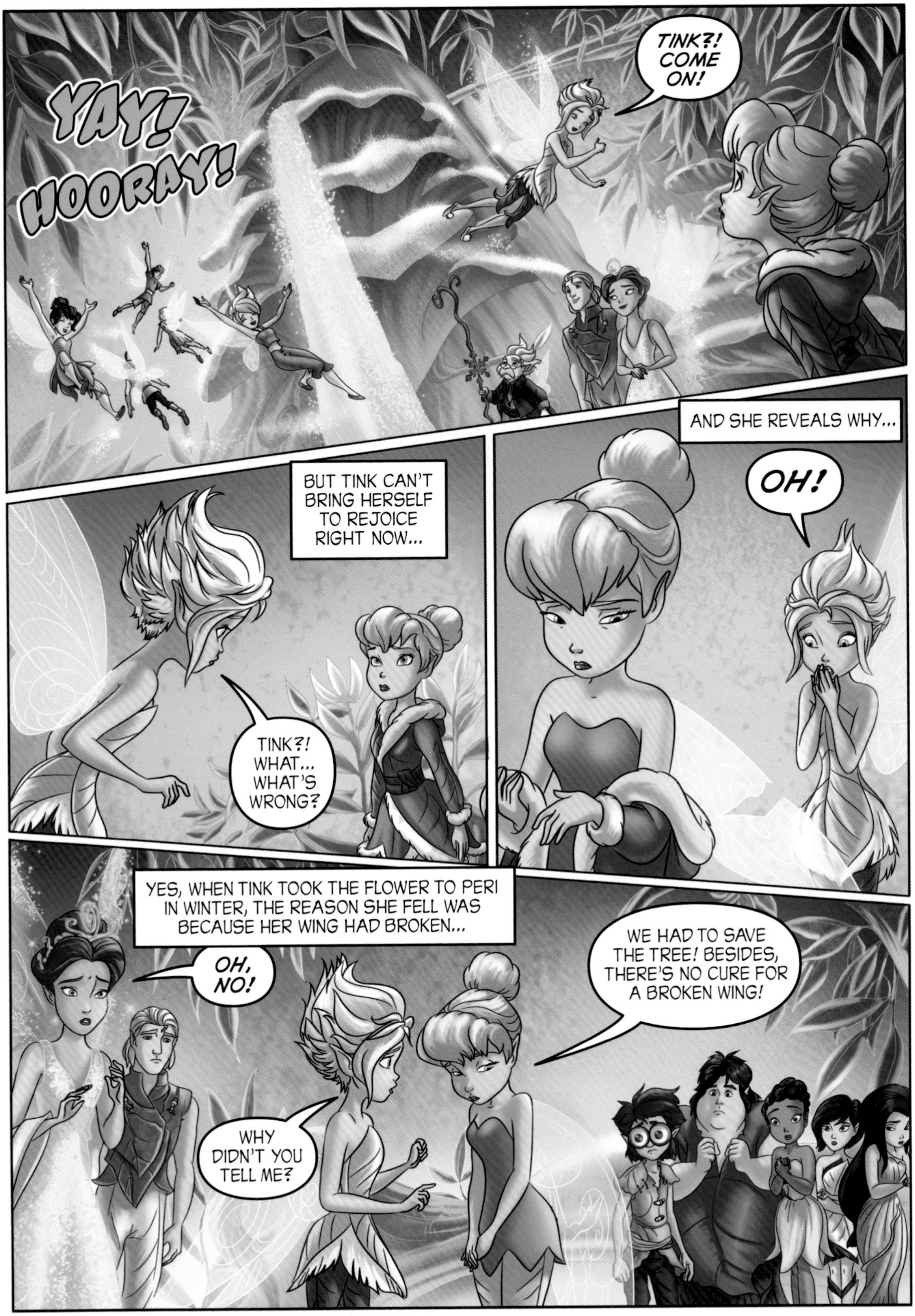
YAY!
HOORAY!
TINK?! COME ON!
AND SHE REVEALS WHY...
BUT TINK CAN'T BRING HERSELF TO REJOICE RIGHT NOW...
TINK?! WHAT... WHAT'S WRONG?
OH!
YES, WHEN TINK TOOK THE FLOWER TO PERI IN WINTER, THE REASON SHE FELL WAS BECAUSE HER WING HAD BROKEN...
OH, NO!
WHY DIDN'T YOU TELL ME?
WE HAD TO SAVE THE TREE! BESIDES, THERE'S NO CURE FOR A BROKEN WING!

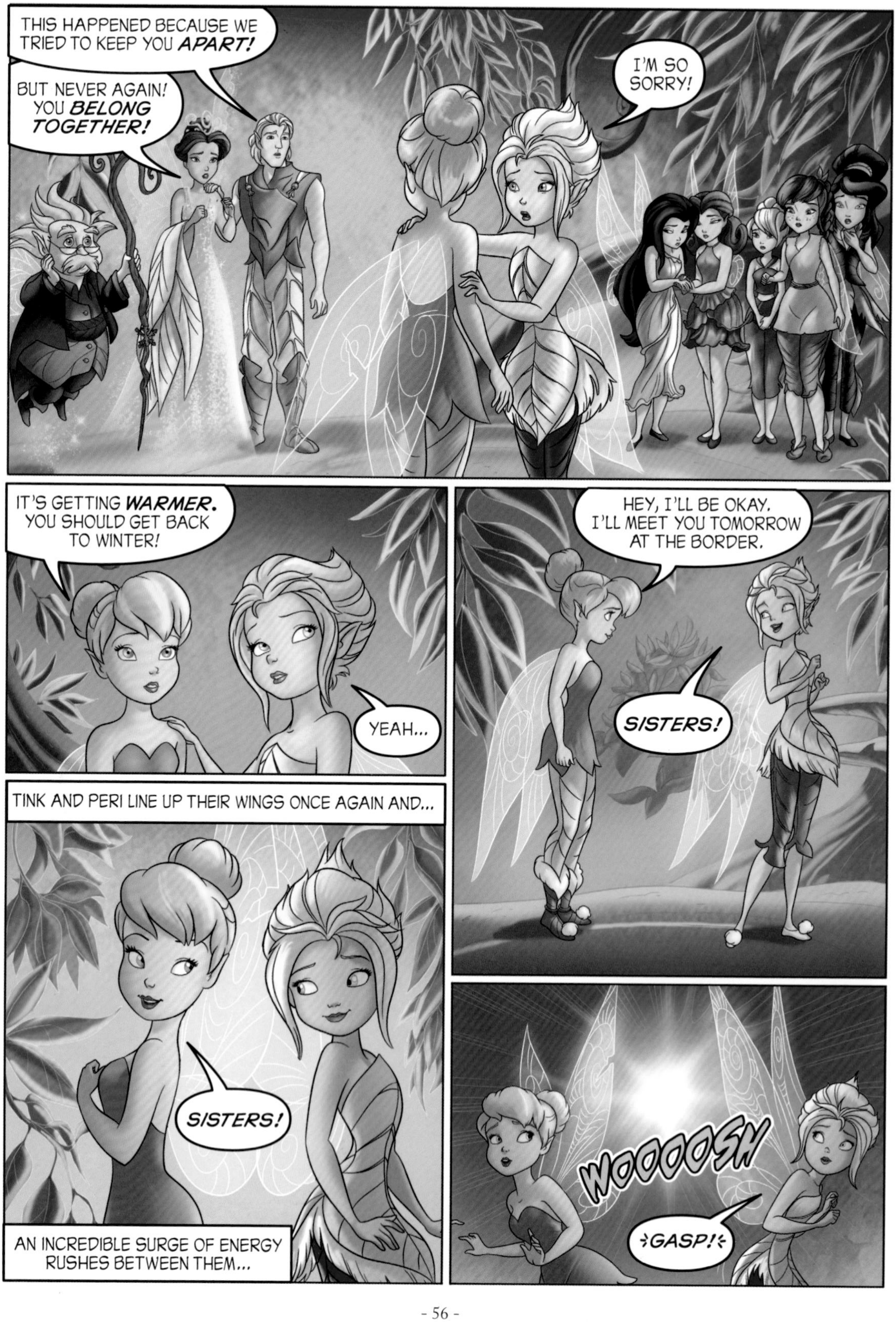
THIS HAPPENED BECAUSE WE TRIED TO KEEP YOU *APART!*
BUT NEVER AGAIN! YOU *BELONG TOGETHER!*
I'M SO SORRY!
IT'S GETTING *WARMER.* YOU SHOULD GET BACK TO WINTER!
YEAH...
HEY, I'LL BE OKAY. I'LL MEET YOU TOMORROW AT THE BORDER.
SISTERS!
TINK AND PERI LINE UP THEIR WINGS ONCE AGAIN AND...
SISTERS!
AN INCREDIBLE SURGE OF ENERGY RUSHES BETWEEN THEM...
WOOOOSH
GASP!

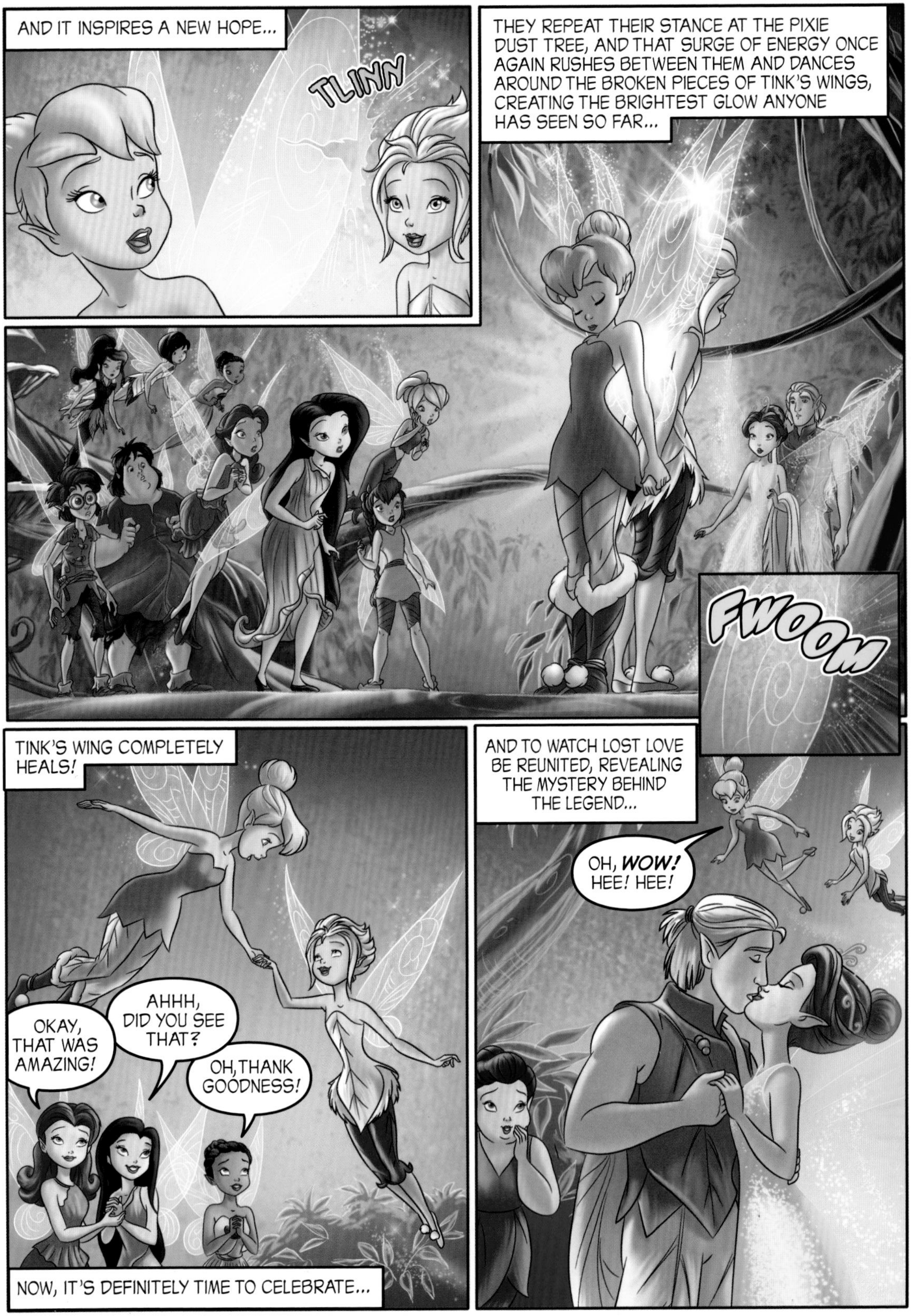
AND IT INSPIRES A NEW HOPE...
TLINN
THEY REPEAT THEIR STANCE AT THE PIXIE DUST TREE, AND THAT SURGE OF ENERGY ONCE AGAIN RUSHES BETWEEN THEM AND DANCES AROUND THE BROKEN PIECES OF TINK'S WINGS, CREATING THE BRIGHTEST GLOW ANYONE HAS SEEN SO FAR...
FWOOM
TINK'S WING COMPLETELY HEALS!
OKAY, THAT WAS AMAZING!
AHHH, DID YOU SEE THAT?
OH, THANK GOODNESS!
NOW, IT'S DEFINITELY TIME TO CELEBRATE...
AND TO WATCH LOST LOVE BE REUNITED, REVEALING THE MYSTERY BEHIND THE LEGEND...
OH, WOW! HEE! HEE!

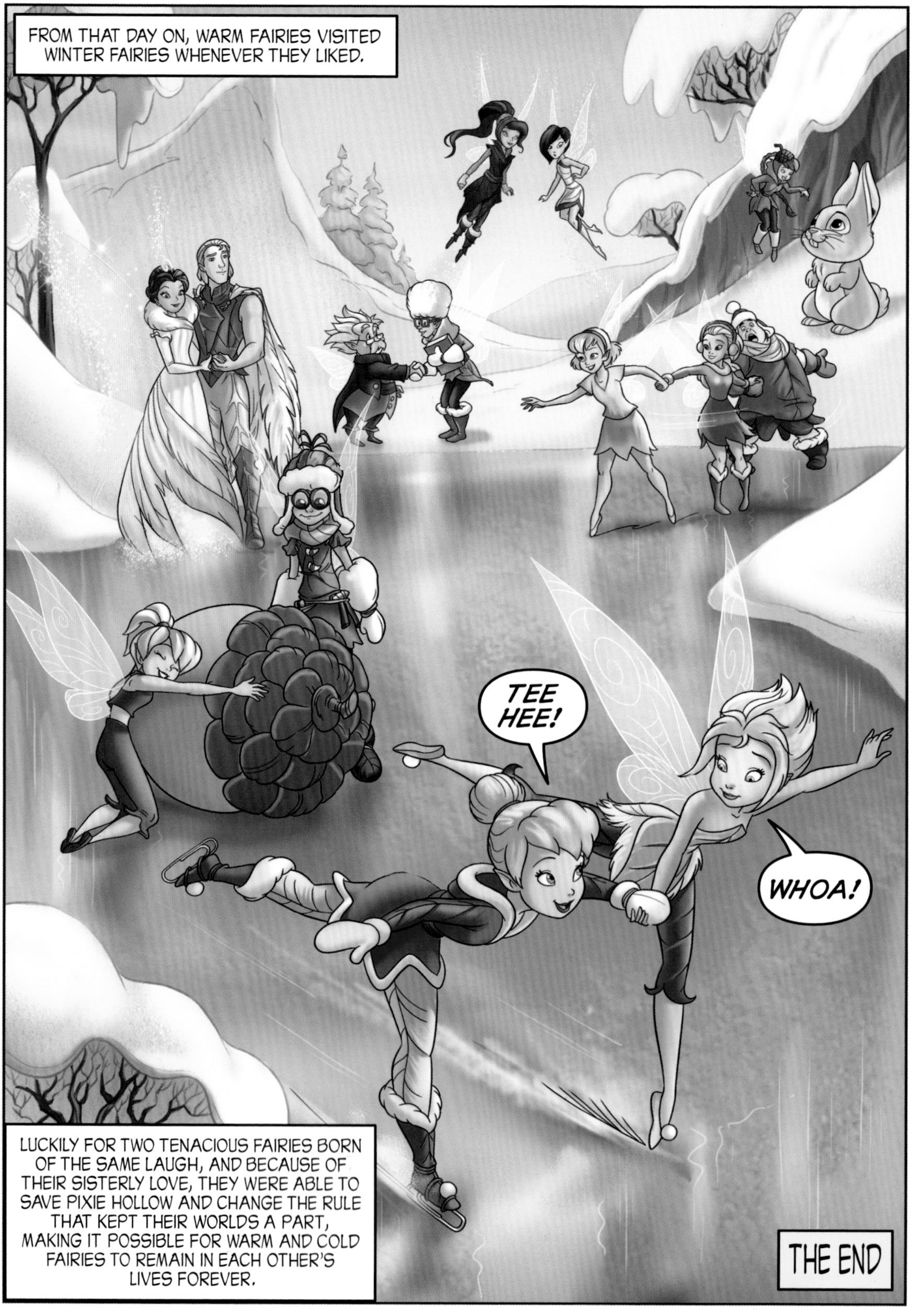
FROM THAT DAY ON, WARM FAIRIES VISITED WINTER FAIRIES WHENEVER THEY LIKED.
TEE HEE!
WHOA!
LUCKILY FOR TWO TENACIOUS FAIRIES BORN OF THE SAME LAUGH, AND BECAUSE OF THEIR SISTERLY LOVE, THEY WERE ABLE TO SAVE PIXIE HOLLOW AND CHANGE THE RULE THAT KEPT THEIR WORLDS A PART, MAKING IT POSSIBLE FOR WARM AND COLD FAIRIES TO REMAIN IN EACH OTHER'S LIVES FOREVER.
THE END

WATCH OUT FOR PAPERCUTZ

Béka and Crip
Dance Class
School Night Fever
PAPERCUTZ
©Bamboo Édition

Welcome to the frozen fifteenth DISNEY FAIRIES graphic novel from Papercutz, those hard-working folks in their over-heated New York City offices dedicated to publishing great graphic novels for all ages! I'm Jim Salicrup, the Editor-in-Chief, who like most everyone in the Northeast this year has been staying indoors, where it's very warm, and venturing outside, where it seems Winter will never end only to see Disney's *Frozen*! Even though it's already Spring, it actually snowed the other day! BRRR!

While a comics adaptation of an animated film can't usually convey everything that was in the original—especially since comics don't have any sound—it is able to capture most of the fun of the actual story. For example, as a long-time fan of Bob Newhart, I'll just imagine his voice saying all of the dialogue for Dewey!

We hope you enjoy the comics adaptation of "The Secret of the Wings" as much as we did! This particular movie seemed to have everything-- all the Disney fairies we love, and Tinker Bell making the most amazing discovery of her life. Not to mention all the humor and adventure we've come to expect from DISNEY FAIRIES.

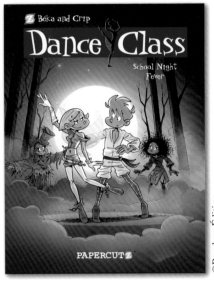

But before I say anymore, I better post a ***SPOILER ALERT*!** If you haven't already seen the DVD or if you're the one person in the world who would actually read this page before the comics, then stop reading this page right now, or it'll spoil the biggest Tinker Bell surprise ever!

There, it should be safe now to talk about Tinker Bell finally finding her sister, Periwinkle, the frost fairy. As a Gemini, I tend to enjoy stories featuring twins, and this one was no exception. After all, who knew Tink even had a sister? Weren't all the fairies of Pixie Hollow in a sense sisters?

In the world of comics, publishers have at times gotten carried away promoting upcoming stories by proclaiming that "Nothing will ever be the same after this!" Well, with such a major new development in Tinker Bell's life, we think we can honestly say, nothing will ever be the same for Tink after this!

And now for something a little different... As you may know, another popular series published by Papercutz is DANCE CLASS, by Béka and Crip, which features the story of three girls, Julia, Alia, and Lucie taking various dance classes. In DANCE CLASS #7 "School Night Fever," Lucie got to dream up and choreograph a dance featuring fairies, and we thought you might enjoy peeking at that story. So, take a look, it appears in just two more pages—as if by magic!

In the meantime, keep believing in "faith, trust, and pixie dust"!

Thanks,

JIM

STAY IN TOUCH!

EMAIL:	salicrup@papercutz.com
WEB:	papercutz.com
TWITTER:	@papercutzgn
FACEBOOK:	PAPERCUTZGRAPHICNOVELS
REGULAR MAIL:	Papercutz, 160 Broadway, Suite 700, East Wing, New York, NY 10038

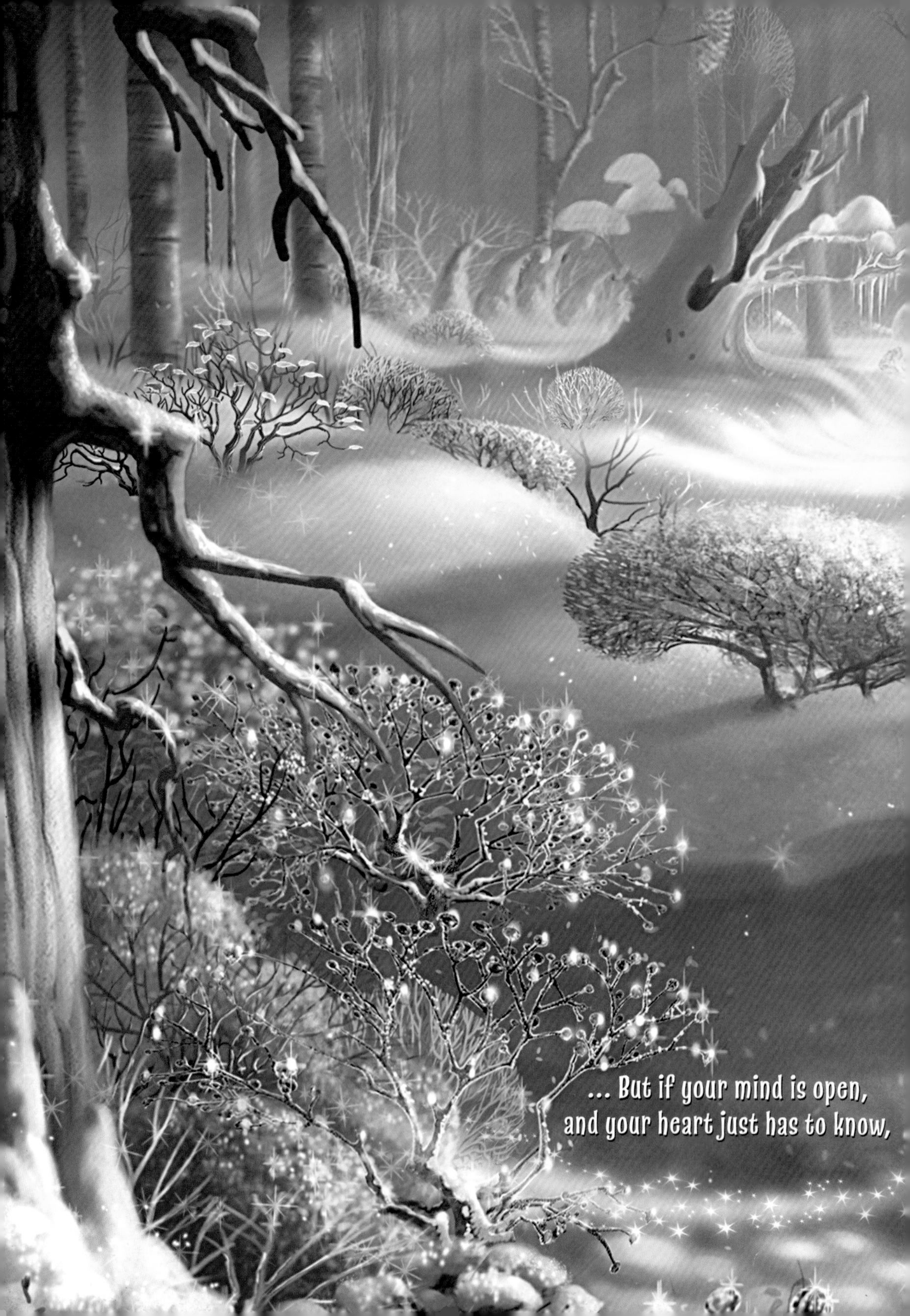

... But if your mind is open,
and your heart just has to know,

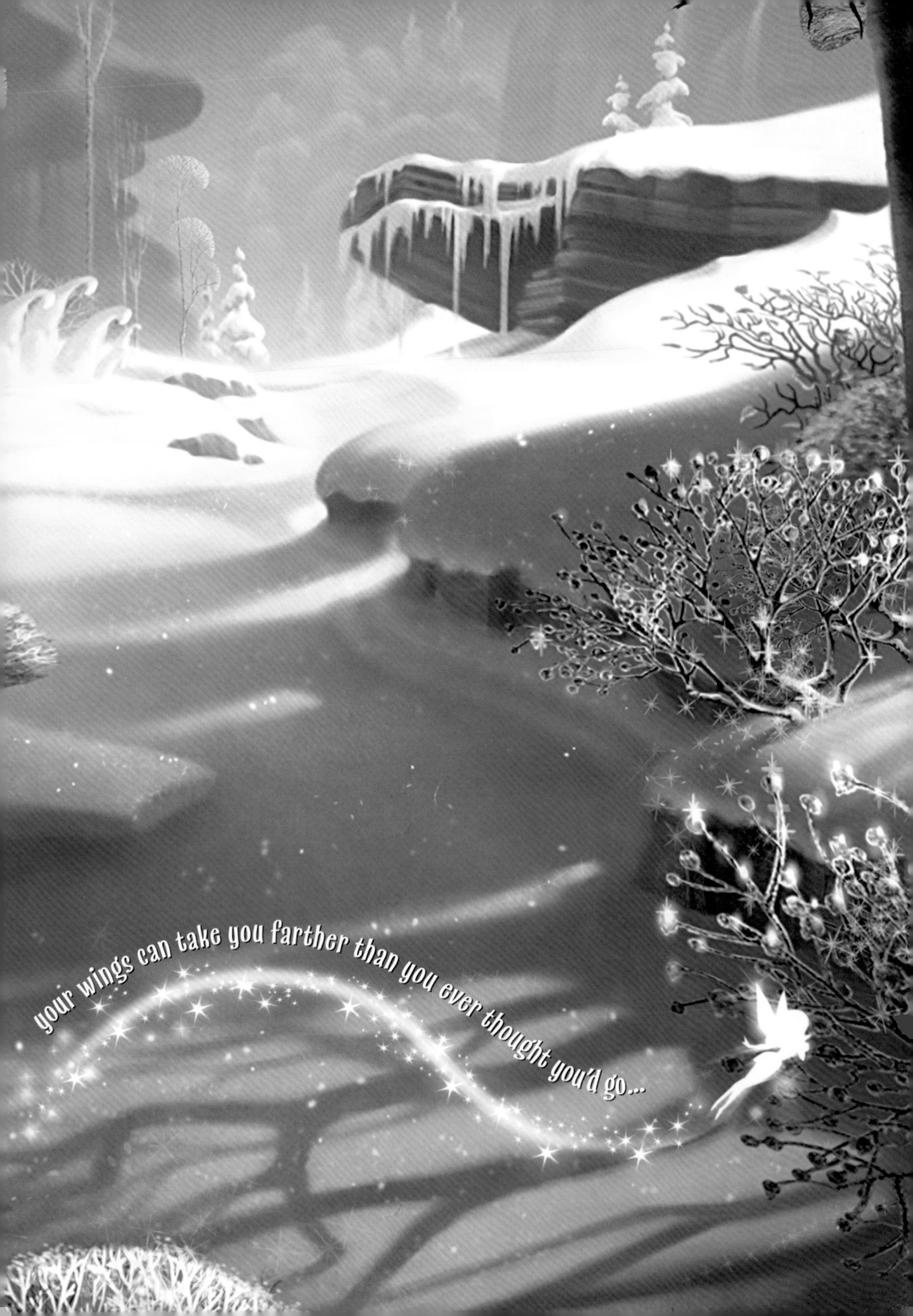
your wings can take you farther than you ever thought you'd go...

A Special Excerpt from DANCE CLASS #7 "School Night Fever"...

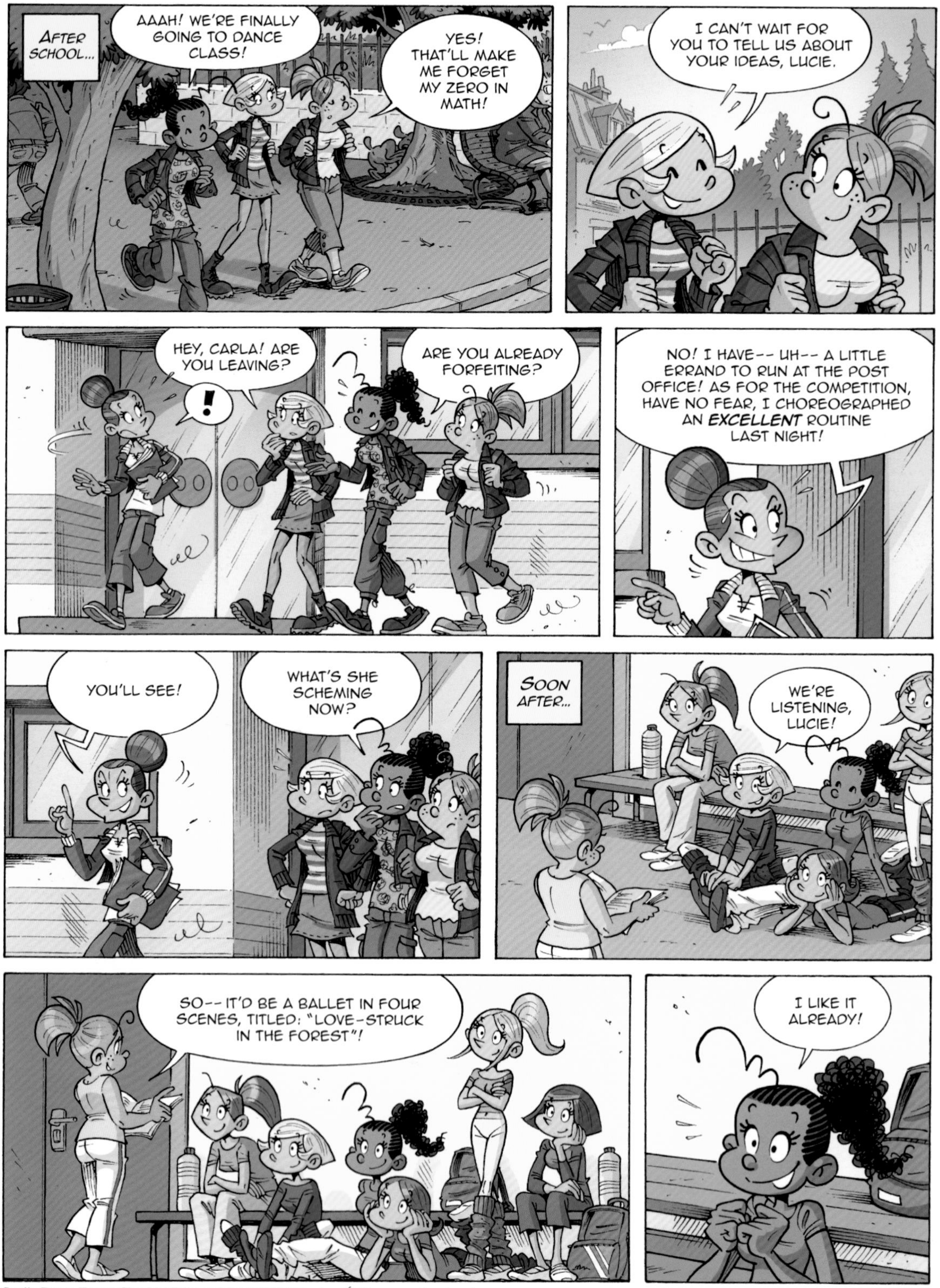
AFTER SCHOOL...
AAAH! WE'RE FINALLY GOING TO DANCE CLASS!
YES! THAT'LL MAKE ME FORGET MY ZERO IN MATH!
I CAN'T WAIT FOR YOU TO TELL US ABOUT YOUR IDEAS, LUCIE.
HEY, CARLA! ARE YOU LEAVING?
!
ARE YOU ALREADY FORFEITING?
NO! I HAVE-- UH-- A LITTLE ERRAND TO RUN AT THE POST OFFICE! AS FOR THE COMPETITION, HAVE NO FEAR, I CHOREOGRAPHED AN EXCELLENT ROUTINE LAST NIGHT!
YOU'LL SEE!
WHAT'S SHE SCHEMING NOW?
SOON AFTER...
WE'RE LISTENING, LUCIE!
SO-- IT'D BE A BALLET IN FOUR SCENES, TITLED: "LOVE-STRUCK IN THE FOREST"!
I LIKE IT ALREADY!

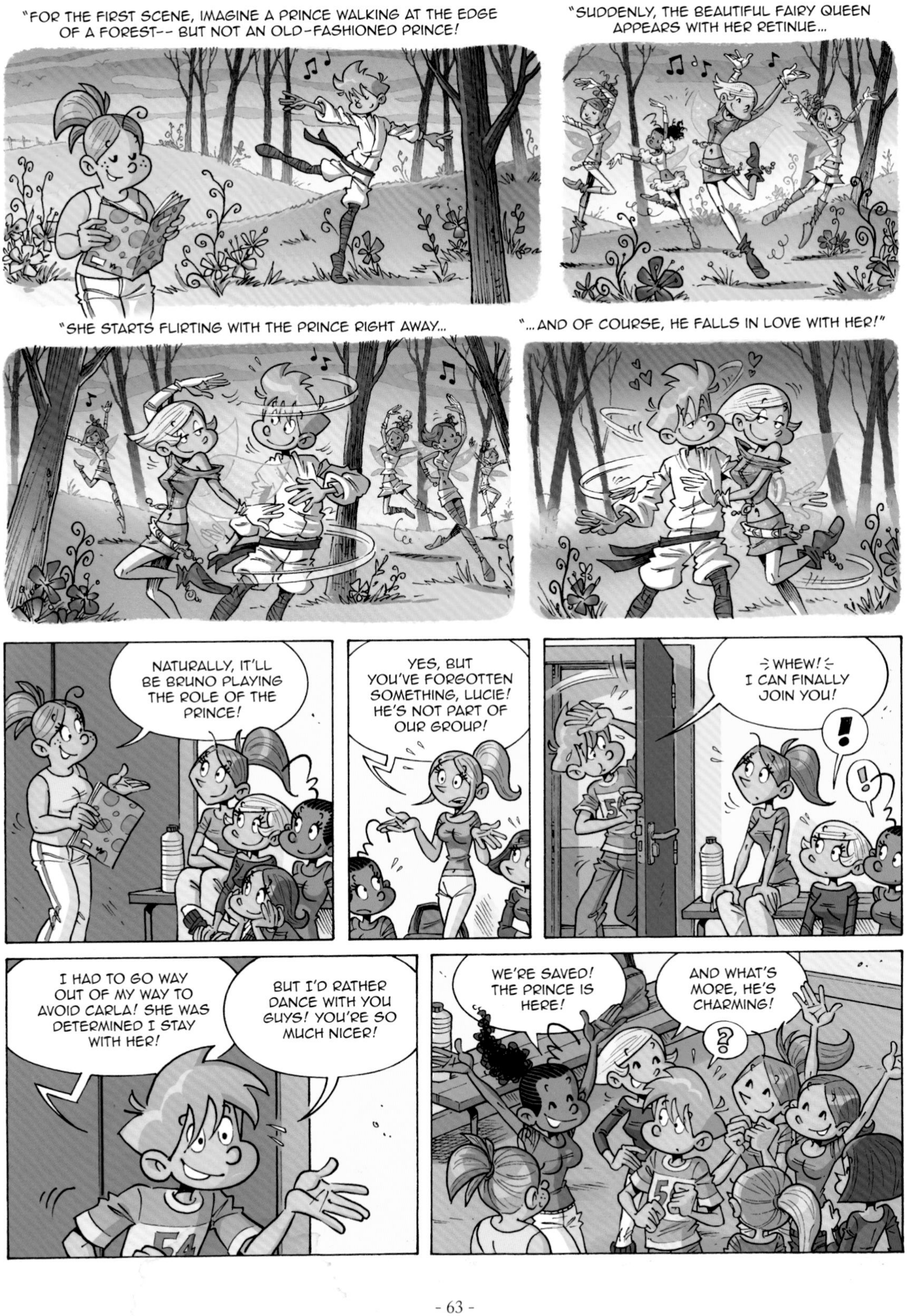

"FOR THE FIRST SCENE, IMAGINE A PRINCE WALKING AT THE EDGE OF A FOREST-- BUT NOT AN OLD-FASHIONED PRINCE!
"SUDDENLY, THE BEAUTIFUL FAIRY QUEEN APPEARS WITH HER RETINUE...
"SHE STARTS FLIRTING WITH THE PRINCE RIGHT AWAY...
"...AND OF COURSE, HE FALLS IN LOVE WITH HER!"
NATURALLY, IT'LL BE BRUNO PLAYING THE ROLE OF THE PRINCE!
YES, BUT YOU'VE FORGOTTEN SOMETHING, LUCIE! HE'S NOT PART OF OUR GROUP!
WHEW! I CAN FINALLY JOIN YOU!
!
!
I HAD TO GO WAY OUT OF MY WAY TO AVOID CARLA! SHE WAS DETERMINED I STAY WITH HER!
BUT I'D RATHER DANCE WITH YOU GUYS! YOU'RE SO MUCH NICER!
WE'RE SAVED! THE PRINCE IS HERE!
AND WHAT'S MORE, HE'S CHARMING!
?

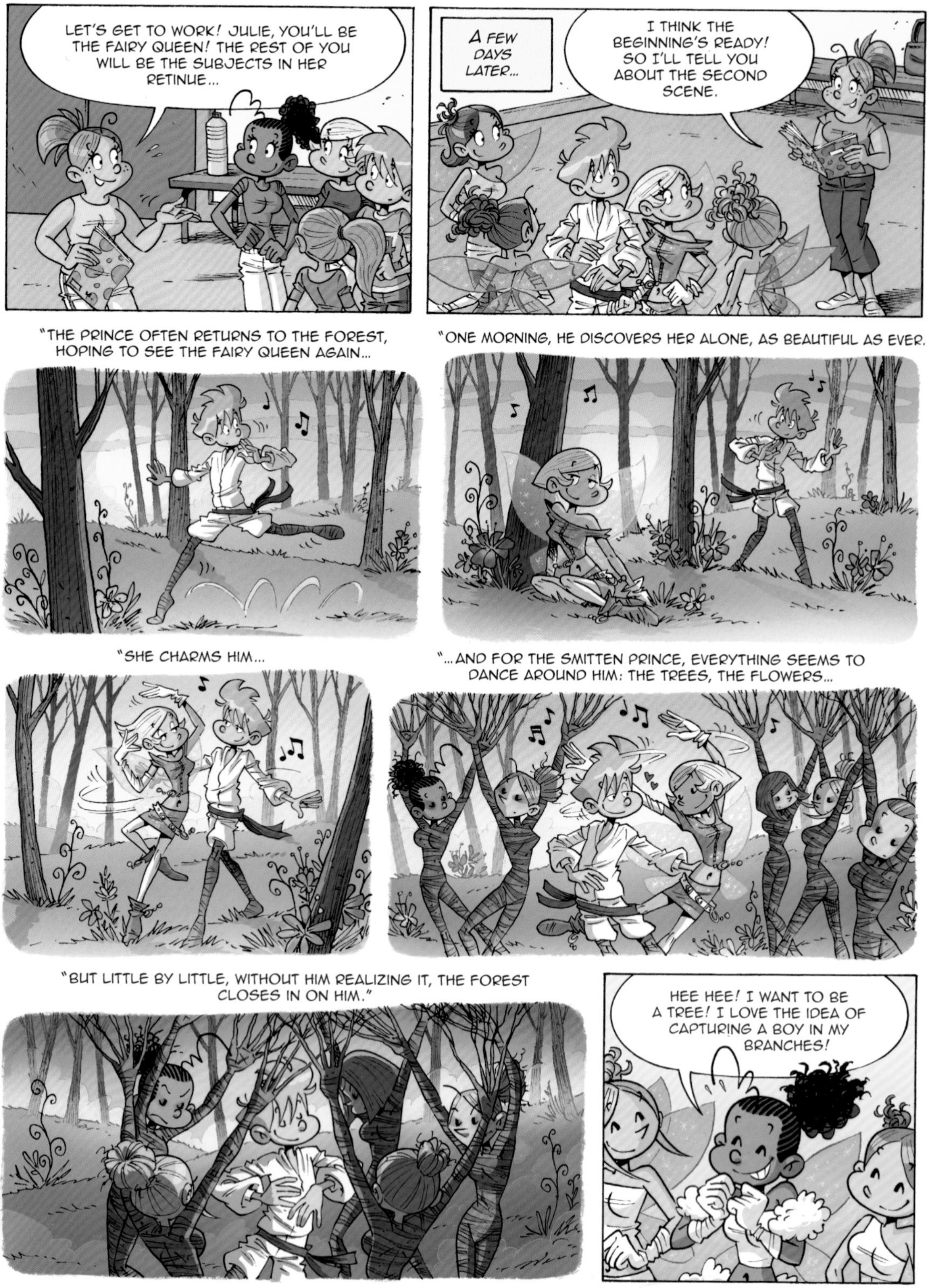
LET'S GET TO WORK! JULIE, YOU'LL BE THE FAIRY QUEEN! THE REST OF YOU WILL BE THE SUBJECTS IN HER RETINUE...
A FEW DAYS LATER...
I THINK THE BEGINNING'S READY! SO I'LL TELL YOU ABOUT THE SECOND SCENE.
"THE PRINCE OFTEN RETURNS TO THE FOREST, HOPING TO SEE THE FAIRY QUEEN AGAIN...
"ONE MORNING, HE DISCOVERS HER ALONE, AS BEAUTIFUL AS EVER.
"SHE CHARMS HIM...
"...AND FOR THE SMITTEN PRINCE, EVERYTHING SEEMS TO DANCE AROUND HIM: THE TREES, THE FLOWERS...
"BUT LITTLE BY LITTLE, WITHOUT HIM REALIZING IT, THE FOREST CLOSES IN ON HIM."
HEE HEE! I WANT TO BE A TREE! I LOVE THE IDEA OF CAPTURING A BOY IN MY BRANCHES!